BC-11603

"He thrived on chaos," her mother had said, and the words had stayed with Catherine. They had had a certain grandeur, then. When the possibility of this long visit had come up, her mother said Harry Ames had, no doubt, changed. "He's a lot older, after all," she said. She had sounded smug, as though age would teach Mr. Ames what everyone else in the world already knew. Her mother had not told her how terrible drinking could be.

PAULA FOX is the award-winning author of many books for young adults, including *The Slave Dancer*, winner of the Newbery Award and a *School Library Journal* Best Book of the Year, and *One-Eyed Cat*, a Newbery Honor Book and an ALA Best Book for Young Adults. Both are available in Dell Laurel-Leaf editions. Ms. Fox lives in Brooklyn, New York.

ALSO AVAILABLE IN LAUREL-LEAF BOOKS:

The Moonlight Man

PAULA FOX

Published by
Bantam Doubleday Dell Books for Young Readers
a division of
Bantam Doubleday Dell Publishing Group, Inc.
1540 Broadway
New York, New York 10036

ISBN: 0-440-20079-2

RL: 5.9

Reprinted by arrangement with Bradbury Press, An Affiliate of Macmillan, Inc.

Printed in the United States of America

April 1988

OPM   17   16   15   14   13   12   11   10   9

FOR MARTIN

The
Moonlight
Man

❧ ❧ ❧ ❧ ❧ ❧ ❧ ❧ **One**

THE SOUND of a flute awakened Catherine Ames. She went from her bed and knelt on the window seat's worn cushion. Her face close to the rusted screen, she listened intently, wondering who it was who walked, playing music, along the narrow street below. But as the music grew fainter, the question that plagued her days rose in her mind. It was like a pain from which only an odd event—a flute played in the middle of the night—could distract her.

Where was he? Where was her father?

She heard a distant flutter of notes; someone banged a window shut. She saw how a strand of moonlight touching the fingers of her hand outspread upon the sill made them ghostly. She felt like a ghost, like nobody's child.

Through no intention of her own, Catherine had overstayed the spring semester at the Dalraida Boarding and Day School by three weeks. The large wood and stone house, which looked from the outside much like the other nineteenth-century mansions in the old Montreal residential neighborhood between Sherbrooke and Ste. Catherine streets, didn't seem like a school since the other seventeen boarding students and eleven day students had left for their summer vacations.

If only that flute player had gone down some other street! She might have slept through the night. It was hard enough to get through the days trying not to look out the window for the postman, trying not to listen constantly for the telephone to ring.

Harry Ames was supposed to have come for her at the end of school and take her back to Rockport, Massachusetts, where he lived with his wife, Emma, and where Catherine was going to spend seven weeks with him, their first long time together since he and her mother had been divorced when she was three years old.

Mr. Ames had not arrived on June 7 when he was expected, nor on the next day or the next. Madame Soule, the director of the school, had telephoned Mr. Ames's Rockport number. Catherine, standing next to Madame, heard the operator say the phone had been temporarily disconnected.

"What am I to do with you, my girl?" Madame had asked, the sympathy in her voice making Catherine even more miserable than she had been on that morning she waited for her father in the school entrance hall, her packed suitcase beside her.

"I think I must send a telegram to your mother," Madame said resolutely. Catherine, trying to be calm, trying not to plead, had persuaded Madame to wait. Her father, she explained carefully, was always late, even for those short visits, themselves so infrequent, which had been their only contact over the last twelve years. She did not tell Madame there had been other occasions when he hadn't turned up at all. But those times had involved the loss of an hour or two with him—not seven weeks. His unexplained absence now was so serious, it made Catherine feel giddy, as though she might faint even as she explained it. What kept her on her feet, kept her from throwing herself into Madame's arms and asking for comfort, was a dogged insistence in herself that he would come.

"I am aware your father is not entirely reliable,"

Madame Soule had said, "but I'm obliged to let your mother know you are still here. It is her right, after all. She did leave you a hotel address in England for emergencies. I think *this* is an emergency, Catherine."

"Not yet," Catherine replied quickly. "You don't know my father."

"But I do know him. I met him before you came to our school. I saw that he was charming, likable. But—" She broke off and shook her head as though in disagreement with some thought she was having. "What if something has happened? His wife might be sick. Anything can happen."

"Someone would let us know," Catherine insisted. "And you don't really know him. But my mother does. She wouldn't think this was an emergency."

Madame scowled ever so slightly. Catherine then told a lie. "Anyhow, Mom isn't at that hotel in Windermere. She and my stepfather went to the Orkneys. She wouldn't get the telegram."

She watched Madame Soule's face intently. If her mother, who wasn't going to the Orkneys until the early part of July, learned Mr. Ames hadn't come to get Catherine, she would fly home to the rescue. And she would never forgive him. Catherine wouldn't be given a chance to spend such a long time with her father until she was old enough to do as she wished.

Madame Soule sighed. "I am sure your mother left a forwarding address in Windermere, too," she said gently. "But—all right, then. We'll give him a few more days."

Triumphant and ashamed, Catherine had gone to her room and unpacked her suitcase. The same day she wrote to her mother in Windermere, telling her she had decided to spend a couple of weeks with a good friend in Toronto before going to her father's in Rockport. It occurred to her that her mother wouldn't believe that—couldn't believe Catherine would give up a moment with her father. What she was counting on was that her mother, only recently married to Carter Beade, had a lot else on her mind. She wrote to the Dalraida student, Betty Jane Rich in Toronto, telling her to keep any letters that might arrive from her mother—she'd explain why in September when school started.

It had all been dreadful, explaining what she didn't understand herself, excusing what she knew to be inexcusable, covering up to gain a few days, and always with her father's unanswering silence. But how much worse to have dragged her mother back at the beginning of her long-delayed honeymoon; how much worse to watch Carter do his I-am-a-patient-wonderful-superior-stepfather routine!

Wasn't it possible that her father had changed his

mind at the last minute, and instead of sending his wife off to Virginia alone to visit her family, had gone with her? But even if Catherine had known Emma's maiden name and where her family lived, she wouldn't have told Madame or tried to track down her father among his in-laws.

Her labors had been in vain; she had tried to freeze everyone as though she'd been *it* in a game of Red Light where each player had to stand still until she stopped looking at him.

The game was over. Madame had said she must wire Catherine's mother. Madame and her husband were leaving for Dijon, France, in a week. Madame LeSueur, the history instructor, and the only teacher still in the house, was going to Rome the next evening. Even the small housekeeping staff was going on vacation. The school would be closed, empty, until the end of August. In September, everyone would know Catherine had been left stranded in school.

But as bad as that would be, it would pass. She did not think she would ever get over her disappointment at her father forsaking her.

She glanced at the clock. It was a minute after midnight, June 28. She turned back to the window, feeling a rush of relief. Giving up made things easier. "What the hell," she said aloud. Maybe her mother would let her fly to England and meet them and go to the Orkneys. When her father finally did show up—if he did—she would be gone.

She stared fiercely at the oriel window on the top floor of the house across the street. From now on, let her father wait on street corners, in restaurants, in hotel lobbies! She caught a flicker of movement. It must be the man who lived there, whom she and her roommate, Cornelia, called the Great Illusion. Sometime last autumn, he had realized they were watching him. He paraded up and down in front of his window, dressed in a plum-colored velvet smoking jacket, waving at them enthusiastically. When the weather was warm, he moved a phonograph to a table where they could see it, played Charles Aznavour records, and danced, throwing them kisses. They had thought him extremely handsome, with his small mustache, his glossy dark hair, and narrow face. One May morning, Cornelia spotted him coming out of the house to the sidewalk. He was so tiny, he would barely have come up to her waist. "Why don't I fly downstairs, grab him, and bring him back up to our eyrie," Cornelia had suggested, and they had laughed wildly and flung themselves about the room. "We shouldn't laugh," one or the other would say, and that would make them laugh even harder.

Now Catherine could see him distinctly as moonlight touched his face. He was looking up at the sky. She could sense he was brooding, awakened perhaps by the flute player, as she had been. His face was in repose, pale as a moth beneath the dark hair. He feels as sad as I do, she thought, wondering why the relief she had felt a few minutes ago didn't seem to matter any longer. She had been almost happy. It was baffling the way feelings changed, each as fleeting as a cat's-paw across the surface of a lake. How she wished she had gone with Cornelia to her home in Dallas! But when Cornelia had invited her, she'd been proud, sure of the summer ahead.

The Great Illusion disappeared from the window. Catherine wandered out into the hall. Silence. Even Roland, Madame's Irish setter, was silent. Usually you had to get to sleep before Roland did or his snoring would keep you up all night. Cornelia claimed that on cold winter nights when Roland slept deeply, he was known to have wakened people in Calgary.

She leaned over the staircase railing, staring down into the darkness. The house smelled stale, hot and faintly syrupy from Madame LeSueur's perfume, or else from the sherry she was said to take baths in. How glad Catherine would have been for Madame LeSueur's amiable company, no matter how much sherry she'd soaked up since five p.m. when she always drank her first little glass.

Catherine's resolution to be patient and stalwart melted away; she felt foolish, ghostly. She'd been pretty good that first week when her father hadn't shown up, not quite as good the second week, and now, at the end of the third week, she didn't feel bad or good, just gone.

She'd dutifully practiced the piano every morning after breakfast. She'd helped Madame Soule with various chores, gone to concerts with Madame LeSueur and listened gravely to her gushing about the divinity of music, her mind elsewhere. She had even dropped in to the badminton and squash club the Dalraida girls belonged to, and she'd discovered that their instructor wasn't drinking tea, as everyone had always assumed, but bourbon from the white coffee cup he kept on a wicker table in the viewing balcony above the courts. Maybe she would laugh about that when she told Cornelia. She had found only a ten-year-old boy to play a badminton set with; she'd beaten him effortlessly and, she admitted to herself, rudely.

"You're mean," he had said to her when he walked away, his badminton racket tucked under a skinny arm. In the evenings she'd played two-handed bridge with Madame LeSueur, whose heavy, jeweled fingers kept her cards in a tight curve. Around ten each evening, after many glasses of sherry, she would stand, lay down her cards in a fan shape on the table, and walk up the stairs to her room with wobbling dignity. Madame Soule never appeared to notice Madame LeSueur's condition, and if Madame Soule's husband, a Scottish lawyer, noticed, he didn't say a word. Cornelia said that Madame Soule's head was so full of grand ideas there was no room in it for ordinary things. She and Catherine joked and laughed about her but they admired her immensely. How she wished Cornelia were here!

She filled her cheeks with air and blew it down into the stairwell. As though in response, a strong smell of the lamb Jeanne had cooked for dinner floated up to her. Oh, she was getting sleepy. . . .

In two days, she would have to be in touch with her mother. She went to her bed and fell on it, knocking the pillow to the floor. Her head felt stuffed with socks. She started up briefly, thinking she heard the faint ring of the telephone from the hall leading to the kitchen. She dragged up the pillow and covered her head with it. Now the phone—if it was a phone—sounded like a bell buoy far out at sea.

Her father loved villages by the sea, islands, rocky headlands. One of her happiest visits with him had taken place on a Saturday when she had expected only lunch and a movie or a walk to the Central Park Zoo. But he had arrived in a rented car and taken her out to the end of Long Island. It was early November and most of the summer people were gone. He had driven over a carpet of hog cranberry right up to a dune and parked there. They got out and both ran down to the edge of the sea.

It was a chilly day with brief moments of sunlight, windy, the sand shadowed by scudding clouds. The great stretch of beach was empty except far ahead, where a young man ran with his dog.

As they trudged through the sand, keeping out of reach of the breaking waves, he told her a story about a man who lived alone in a lighthouse with no telephone. He had had an attack of appendicitis and set out in agony for the nearest village, several miles away. In the dark night, close to death, he struggled on, draining the poison out of himself. By the time he reached help, he was out of danger. She wondered if the story could be true. She knew her father would say a story was always true in some way, even if it wasn't factual and couldn't be proved. Facts, he had said to her, could lead in any direction you wanted them to, but there was only one truth.

What truth was that? she mused, and musing, fell asleep. Almost at once she was awake. The overhead light was on. Madame Soule, wrapped in her long, green silk dressing gown, was standing beside the bed shaking her shoulder.

"Catherine, your father is on the telephone."

Catherine staggered up.

"Let him wait a minute," Madame said with a certain sharpness. "He's kept you waiting a very long time. You're still asleep. Wake up entirely or you'll trip on the stairs."

Behind Madame stood Roland, his leash gripped firmly between his jaws. "Don't be ridiculous, Roland," said Madame. "It's one o'clock in the morning." Roland groaned through the leash. "Night has no meaning for this creature," Madame remarked. She looked as though she had more to say but Catherine didn't wait to hear. Her bathrobe thrown over her shoulders, she ran out of the room and down the two flights of stairs to the hall, where she grabbed up the telephone.

"Daddy?"

"I'm sorry, sorry, sorry—you can't know how badly I feel," he said.

"But what happened?"

"Catherine, I wasn't fit to be around. I'm afraid I lifted a few too many glasses in my wretchedness. The first blow was a perfectly terrible row with Emma. She didn't want to horn in on us and our plans, but she discovered a cousin she detests is going to be in Petersburg while she's visiting her family.

Like a lot of peaceable women, she's wild when she's crossed—"

"You could have telephoned or written," Catherine interrupted.

"I did telephone a week ago, dear Rabbit. A Tuesday evening, I think. I spoke to a person so swoggled I thought I'd been connected with your local loony bin. I shouted my name at her—and yours—but all she wanted to do was to talk about Mozart—or perhaps it was Moss Hart—it was hard to tell."

She remembered that Tuesday Madame Soule and her husband had taken her to see a new ballet company. Madame LeSueur must have consumed more of her sherry than usual and imagined the phone call was from another music lover.

"You could have written," she said.

"I know I could have written—but every day it seemed the damn clouds would blow away and things would settle down and I'd be able to come and get you."

"It's all right," she said suddenly, though she had meant to press him more, make him really answer her. But she didn't want to have to think any longer about how unhappy she'd been.

"I know," he said. "I know you don't want to hear all this, but you must. Later it will matter. I also had trouble with a series of articles that bored me to death to write—and the editor hated them! So, of course, I defended them with three times more self-righteousness than if I'd *liked* writing them— Emma, at least, was mollified. I sent her off to Charleston for a week. The cousin's only stay-ing—"

"I'm so glad you phoned," Catherine interrupted him again, nearly out of breath, as though it had been she doing all the talking.

"Okay. I'll stop," he said. "You deserve to call the turns. Wait till you see the funny little house I've rented. It sits on the edge of a cliff. You can't actually hear the sea but it's not far."

Catherine heard faint noises from the other side of the kitchen where the household staff lived. The smell of roast lamb was much stronger down here, faintly sickening. She resolved to ask him no more questions. He sounded so apologetic, and so glad to talk to her. She didn't want to reproach him any more. But before she could stop herself, a question burst out of her.

"Why couldn't I have come to Rockport?"

"Oh—my suspicious girl! So that's it! Here's the reason. Emma and I are thinking of moving to Nova Scotia. The whole coast around Rockport has be-come simply overrun with tourists and commerce, and in the summer, if I want to buy a loaf of bread, I must dress up in Alpine gear to climb through the crowds. So I thought to combine our visit with a look around a bit of the Maritime Provinces. Have you got that straight? Will you remember all that I'm about to tell you—how to find the Digby ferry when you get off the train? How to order a cup of tea and practice up for the day when you'll sit in the salon of a great ship? If there are any great ships left. . . . And as the ferry draws into Digby harbor, you will see a portly, distinguished figure on the wharf. It will be me, your dear papa. . . ."

She laughed as she always did when he described himself mockingly.

"I'll wire you some change in the morning so you'll have enough money for tickets and for those magazines girls of fifteen are supposed to crave. By the way, I have a stack of letters from your mother to you. Is she visiting every hamlet in Cumberland and Westmoreland? Did she marry a census taker?"

"Where are you phoning from?" she asked hurriedly.

There was silence, then a roaring as though a wave had broken over the telephone. "From the bottom of the sea?" she whispered anxiously, fearful that he might have gone away.

"Are you running a detective agency on the

side?"His voice came on strongly; she heard laughter in it. "Some things must remain mysteries," he said, adding in his most serious voice, "I'm so glad we're going to have this time, Catherine, though in my usual fashion I've spoiled some of it."

After he'd told her about getting to the ferry and what time he'd expect her on the Nova Scotia side —"though I'll wait for every boat until you appear"—they said good-bye and she stood in the hall for a while, astonished at how everything had changed. Yet she had known he'd turn up, hadn't she?

She went into the living room that ran the length of the house and sat down in front of the grand piano, lifting her hands up high as though about to play a great smashing chord. She let them drop down so lightly her fingers barely rested on the keys. The room smelled of lemon furniture polish and of Madame LeSueur's French cigarettes which she thought no one knew she smoked. Catherine realized suddenly how safe she felt in that room.

It had been difficult, frightening, to leave her mother, her life in New York, her friends there, and come to another country—*almost* another country. She'd made it even more foreign for herself by liking a French Canadian, Philippe Petit, a sophomore at

McGill University, more than anyone except Cornelia. Her mother continued to be slightly suspicious of Dalraida because, Catherine was pretty sure, her father had chosen it. If her mother hadn't been so caught up with Carter a year and a half ago, Mr. Ames might have had more difficulty persuading her to let Catherine come to Montreal. She was turning into a New York City hick, her father had written her mother, who had shown the letter to Catherine. He would pay for absolutely everything, he had said, including an eyelash curler, if Catherine went in for such things. She needed to get away from New York—and it was important to learn another language, other ways. Catherine wanted to do what her father wanted her to do. In time, her mother yielded. She had met Madame Soule and that had helped, although she'd observed that Madame was rather an unconventional type to be running a girls' school.

Catherine stood up, exhilarated at the thought of the weeks ahead of her, and ran up the stairs. As she passed Madame Soule's room, she heard Roland snoring, and she imagined telling her father stories about the dog. Madame insisted he was a great hunter. When the school went up to their ski cabin in the Laurentian Mountains, she took the girls on long walks, during which she would occasionally halt and shout, "Point!" at poor Roland. The dog would wag his tail, look up at his mistress with his slightly crossed eyes, and sit down. Or else he would turn sideways to the direction of Madame's pointing finger. You could say, of course, that he pointed with his rib cage.

As Catherine passed the closed bedroom doors, she thought fleetingly of the other students: tough Emily and her humble roommate, Little Jane, who did whatever Emily told her to do and had given up knitting angora sweaters because Emily declared angora was disgusting and sentimental; then Margo Berry, who shared a room with two other girls— Margo, the Westport vamp, her hair falling all over her face, with more clothes than any two other students, who wore a perfume she wouldn't reveal the name of and which she kept so well hidden no one had been able to find it, despite endless searches when she was out; then, on the top floor, across from Catherine and Cornelia, the only student who had a room to herself, a thin, tall girl named Gabrielle, who wore a ratty fur jacket instead of goose down, and high heels. She had a damp, uncertain voice. No one seemed to like her much, partly because she spoke French so perfectly—she'd spent most of her life in Europe. Her mother had appeared twice at the school, once with a man she introduced as a Hungarian count. His name was unpronounceable. The girls referred to him as Dracula. The second time she'd taken Gabrielle out of the school for good in April. Then she turned up with a sunburned young man who looked like a tennis player. It had been hard to be pleasant to Gabrielle. She was at once so meek and so haughty. Yet Catherine felt, reluctantly, that they had more in common with each other than with the other students, whose parents behaved predictably—unlike Gabrielle's mother and her own father. When Harriet Blacking, one of Margo's roommates, began to bully Gabrielle, Catherine had found it a little easier to be friendly to her.

Harriet Blacking was the dark presence in the school, a rather small girl, plump, nearly neckless, with dead-white skin and the thinnest nose Catherine had even seen, as thin as the blade of a pocketknife. Harriet always had the goods on someone. Everyone was afraid of her except tough Emily, who used to kick her if she came too close. The odd thing was, Emily seemed to amuse Harriet.

Her thoughts about Harriet made her uneasy, as though Harriet would somehow know she'd been peached in Dalraida for three weeks. Where *had* her father been phoning from? And what was it he and Emma had quarreled about? Had Emma wanted to come with them to Nova Scotia after all?

She wasn't going to think about Harriet, or Emma. She began to pack her suitcase, right then at two in the morning.

✈ ✈ ✈ ✈ ✈ ✈ ✈ ✈ Two

THE DIRT ROAD along which Catherine drove the station wagon was deeply rutted and so narrow that wild bramble scratched the car's sides. She stayed in first gear, feeling the weight of the massive metal box in her hands as it lunged forward.

"I've resigned myself to respectability," her father had said when he led her to the car in Digby. He had taught her to drive two years earlier in a small, bright foreign model on a country lane near White Plains, and when she asked what had happened to it, he said, "A last youthful squeal. I gave it up This monster is my future."

The monster stalled. Catherine's jaw ached from being clenched.

"Let her sit a sec, Missy," said the farmer, Mr Glimm, who sat in the front with her. He had grown sober during the last hour, like someone rising slowly from the bottom of a pond. He needn't have spoken so softly. The two men in the back seat, her father and Mr. Conklin, a local bus driver, were sleeping snoring loudly but not in unison. It was nearly five a.m. Catherine was taking her father's friends home

"Try now," urged Mr. Glimm.

The car started up at once and shot forward "Downshift!" Mr. Glimm directed her. She caugh a glimpse of his unshaven chin, heavy and slack above his tightly buttoned wool shirt.

The bramble fell away, the thick oak wood behind it thinned. She saw how the light had changed; the sky was no longer black as it had been when she had started out from the backyard of the little house but a pale and blistered gray. There was a gleam o black water to her right. Mist rose from its surface and hooked onto the branches of a dead tree like cotton caught on pins.

"There's our marsh," the farmer said. "Not much farther for me, half a mile or so. . . ."

She gripped the wheel and leaned forward to peer through the windshield and the sliding clumps of damp leaves that clung to the glass.

"My pals from the village are coming," Mr. Ames had announced when he left her after supper to drive in to Mackenzie and pick them up. She hadn't much wanted to meet anyone. She'd been in Nova Scotia for two days. When she saw two middle-aged men getting out of the car in the yard, she felt her father was elbowing her aside. All three men began to drink at once.

She had seen her father drink before. When they had a restaurant meal, it was always in a place that served liquor. He usually ordered whiskey in a tall glass with a little water and no ice. She had never seen such drinking as she had last night.

The bottles Mr. Ames had bought at the government-run liquor store were lined up on the kitchen counter. The three men emptied them as though it had been their duty to do so.

Years ago, when her mother still talked about her father, she had told Catherine that wherever they lived when they were married, he managed to find all the local rats. Catherine guessed he had searched out the rats of Mackenzie before she'd gotten off the Digby ferry, though Farmer Glimm was more like a badger.

"Up there," he muttered. "Up on the rise."

The marsh had given way to solid land. The farmhouse on the hill looked desolate. If there had not been a light in a window, she would have thought no one lived there. A large dog came from behind an outbuilding and silently raced down the hill. Catherine turned off the motor.

Her father groaned. Mr. Conklin woke up and began to whistle, as though to show how lighthearted he felt. He broke off to emit a high-pitched giggle. A woman was moving slowly toward them. The dog ran back and forth between her and the car. The woman's hair hung down from her head in two long thin braids. She wore a thick shawl over a faded lilac flannel nightgown. When she was a yard away from the car, she halted and stared, her face expressionless.

Farmer Glimm sighed and fumbled with the door handle. Without looking at the woman, he bobbed his head at Catherine.

"My missus," he murmured, as though to himself. "Just keep on going," he said in a louder voice. "Don't go back the way we come. This road will take you straight to Mackenzie. And thank you, Missy." His wife clutched her shawl so tightly, Catherine could see the outline of her shoulder bones. With the dog prancing about them, the two people went up the rise toward the farmhouse. They didn't speak as far as Catherine could tell.

"Well done!" Mr. Ames called out from the back seat. "I taught you good. Doesn't she drive like a champion, Mr. Conklin?"

"She does," Mr. Conklin squeaked.

Catherine didn't turn around. She started up the car. The silence of the farmer's wife had been full of anger. As though he had read her mind, her father said, "Serves that woman right—waiting up for him like Nurse Sally. My God! We need a vacation from women."

"Right," agreed Mr. Conklin.

She had not dreamt people could drink as they had, pouring the liquor down their throats as though they were trying to drown themselves. When Catherine, growing frightened, disgusted by them, had left the parlor and gone into the kitchen hoping to find some chore to do, her father had shouted, "They want to catch you in their domestic webs. They want to bring a man down."

Standing in the dark kitchen, her fists clenched, Catherine had hated him. How could it be that only two days earlier she had packed her suitcase, thinking she was about to embark on a splendid journey?

The journey had taken her to a dinky parlor, and the sight of her father, a shambling wreck crashing into furniture, reciting snatches of poetry to tall, silly Mr. Conklin and the short, melancholy farmer.

"You mus' drive us, my dear girl," her father had said at last. "I've not the knack at the moment. You mus' drive us. . . ."

As she gained the road, she felt his hand on the back of her neck. She shook it off.

"Ah, well. I can hardly blame you," he said plaintively.

"Leave me off outside Mackenzie," Mr. Conklin said, with the self-importance of a foolish man. He neighed suddenly like a horse. "It's a treat to have someone else do the driving for a change," he said. "But don't go no further. I got to get home without no one seeing me. Saves the nerves."

She stopped the car just before the dirt road joined the blacktop, the one she remembered from the shopping she and her father had done yesterday. She kept her eyes straight ahead. The car door opened; there were muttered farewells. Her father said, "A fine evening, lad. We'll do it again." He spoke as though challenging her.

They wouldn't do it again with her around, she told herself. She had enough money to buy a return ticket to Montreal. Madame Soule would help her. Maybe she would visit Betty Jane Rich in Toronto. And her mother would be back at the end of July.

She would not see her father again. Perhaps she would speak to him on the telephone. She might even write him a letter now and then over the years. "He thrived on chaos," her mother had said, and the words had stayed with Catherine. They had had a certain grandeur, then. When the possibility of this long visit had come up, her mother said Harry Ames had, no doubt, changed. "He's a lot older, after all," she said. She had sounded smug, as though age would teach Mr. Ames what everyone else in the world already knew. Her mother had not told her how terrible drinking could be.

She reversed the car violently. Her father let out a wordless exclamation and fell back against the seat. She was glad. In the rearview mirror, she could see Mr. Conklin walking along the road, a tall, rather frail-looking man huddled over himself.

By the time she parked in the yard, her father was asleep again. She opened the door quietly and went to the house, leaving him in the car. For a little while, sitting on the hard, knobby horsehair sofa in the parlor, she felt the force of a loneliness she'd never experienced before.

He had made her such a good supper; he had watched her eat with such unconcealed delight. "You didn't know I could cook, did you?" he had asked. "I'm full of surprises."

He had talked about his life, the early days before he'd met and married her mother. He told her he'd been thrown out of two colleges for what he proudly called "riotous behavior," and how he'd shipped out on a freighter to Valparaiso and read Joseph Conrad's novels all the way there and back. He described the ways he made a living—once he'd put an ad in a Boston newspaper when he was living in Provincetown, saying he could read people's futures in their faces. He'd gotten tons of photographs, he said. "My God! I had to leave town. But I couldn't bring myself to throw away all those pictures. I still have some of them in a box somewhere; they're fading now, as the people have—their futures all caught up with them at last." He talked about books he loved, and poets, and countries where he had lived.

"You're like Scheherazade," Catherine had said.

He smiled and replied, "Yes, yes. I'm talking against the time of the executioner, too."

He was quiet as she put away the dried dishes, but he walked restlessly around the small kitchen. After a while, he said, almost coldly, as though speaking of a person he didn't particularly care for, "I didn't have the endurance for it. So I write travel books. Not the way Conrad did."

Then he had gone to Mackenzie to get Mr. Conklin, and to the farm to pick up Mr. Glimm.

Did he drink so much when Emma was around? Was this to be that vacation from women he'd shouted at her about in a hard, sorrowful voice? What about her, his daughter? Was she merely an excuse to get away from Emma?

She suddenly realized why he hadn't come to get her at the school, or written, or tried to call more than once. He'd been drinking the way he had tonight, making himself insensible, escaping from reason and obligation. Struck down all at once by exhaustion, Catherine fell asleep sitting up on the sofa.

She woke to see a sash of sunlight across her cotton skirt and, sleepily, stretched her hand to feel its warmth. Her father was sitting in a chair across from her, staring at her. When she looked up at him, he smiled. He looked terrible, pale and blotchy, his eyes sunken. But his smile was so tender, she felt her indignation slip away.

"I was so scared," she blurted out, and felt that to be a deeper truth than her anger at him.

"Of course you were," he said. "But you were a model of competence. Driving that heap of tin around dirt roads in the middle of the night."

"You were like drunk bears. I didn't know what you might do. . . ."

"Bears," he repeated meditatively. "Bears have a stench that makes strong men weep."

"And they're dangerous," she said.

"*Men* are dangerous," he said. He stood up, the ratty tweed jacket he called his Italian cad outfit straining its last button over his bulky chest and big belly. "Men *like* to be dangerous," he added, as if to himself.

He ducked his head suddenly so that it nearly rested on his shoulder, and he rubbed his hands together like a fly. "Forgive me, little child. Forgive my wickedness, won't you?"

She willed herself not to laugh. She knew he was taking advantage of her. Then she heard her own involuntary little bark of laughter.

He looked cheerful at once. "Look," he said, holding out his hands. "See how the poor things tremble? You'll have to shave me before Mrs. Landy gets here. Don't be mad at me. I've got the humblies."

"Humblies?" she asked coldly.

"That's when you long to be forgiven for your vileness by every living creature," he explained. He grinned at her. He seemed to know he'd won her over, no matter how she sounded, and he didn't mind showing her he knew. "It's when you feel you're Uriah Heep's younger brother, Disgusting Heep," he said.

"I don't know how to shave someone," she said.

"Yes, you do," he replied. "The knowledge of shaving is deep in you. Women are a race of barbers."

"You forgot to put on socks," she observed, suddenly noticing his bare ankles.

"That's not all I forgot," he said. She stared at his narrow ankles and slender feet. She thought—that's a part of him that is still young, the way he was years ago, before the belly and the graying blond hair and all the lines in his face.

"You weren't dangerous. You were soggy lumps," she said, and worried that she'd gone too far. She couldn't recall, now that she thought about it, seeing him angry, not at her in any case.

"Yes, it's strange, isn't it," he said in the thoughtful, serious voice that she loved. "We drink to be dangerous and end up soggy lumps."

He reached out across the space between them, his hand moving through sunlight until it touched her knee, which he patted.

"I'm going to fix you a wonderful breakfast as soon

as I can hold a cup without dropping it. You'll see! A perfect egg, fried ever so delicately in butter, and toast caving in with honey. But first—if you'd make me some coffee. It'll give me strength."

She knew one thing about him, the way he talked about what he was going to do as though the words fed a hope always at risk of fading.

She made him coffee and watched him drink it as he leaned against the sink. She felt he was returning to her from a long way away. He looked back at her over the rim of his cup. In the musty little kitchen, in the silence, he appeared to be pondering something. Was it because he wasn't talking that she suddenly felt so strongly the reality of where she was?

After he had finished the coffee, he said he'd devised a plan for shaving. He'd be more at ease in the bathtub and therefore less likely to start involuntarily with terror when confronting a woman with a razor in her hand.

"You sound as if you think men and women are enemies," she said.

"I suppose you think they're not?" he asked, with an edge of hardness.

"Women don't go to war."

"You must read up on the Amazons."

"They're a myth."

He started to reply but smiled mildly instead. As she followed him up the narrow staircase to the bathroom, he said, over his shoulder, "You're pretty tough yourself."

He stepped right into the tub, gripping its sides as he lowered himself until he was reclining against the curved back. She picked up his straight razor which lay among some toilet articles on a shelf.

"Soap first, for mercy's sake!" he groaned.

"I don't want to do this," she said. She didn't want to be tough, either, not in the way she thought he'd meant. He had put a bent cigarette in his mouth and was fumbling in his pockets for a match.

"Put that away," she said indignantly.

"All right, all right—never mind the evil of tobacco. Mrs. Landy will be scandalized if I look like the bum I am. Get on with it now!"

What if Mrs. Landy, the woman Mr. Ames had hired to keep house for them, and who lived in a hamlet several miles east, crept up the stairs and saw Catherine with a razor in her hand and Mr. Ames in the tub? She managed to stir up some lather with a sliver of soap and tepid water. She knelt and covered his cheeks and chin with it.

He was fifty years old. She was not accustomed to being so close to an adult man. Her stepfather hugged her "hello" or "good-bye" so quickly she had not really seen his face except when he moved away from her, and Philippe was nineteen and his skin was smooth and taut. He could never become so fragile, so old, as her father was, lying there in the old tub, its claw feet sunk into linoleum that might once have been green, his eyes bloodshot, his skin the color of an oyster.

"Come on," he ordered her. "I'll pray silently so as not to unnerve you."

She held the razor just above his face. He gave her a look of mock terror. She held her breath and drew the blade down across a stubble of whiskers.

"I didn't cut you," she said triumphantly.

"Admirable child," he said, in what he called his humbug voice and which he used, she knew, when he wanted her to laugh and not to think too hard about what he was up to.

When she had finished, he climbed out of the tub slowly, groaning and complaining. He wiped his face carelessly with the sleeve of his pajama top that hung from a hook on the back of the door; then he peered into a small mirror nailed up over the wash-basin.

"Very good," he observed.

"I missed a lot of places," she said.

He made a large gesture with his hand, waving

away any objections. "Survival is what we're after," he said, "not perfection." With a sudden excess of energy, he hurried out of the bathroom and down the stairs, calling back to her that it was time for her reward.

Catherine went to her room to change her clothes. The first thing she saw, on the windowsill where she'd left it, was the pile of letters from her mother which he'd handed her without comment when she arrived.

She felt a touch of guilt. She'd read only three of them. There were probably more now in Toronto, at Betty Jane Rich's house. She must write to her mother in Windemere today and tell her everything was fine. Catherine laughed out loud.

The egg was a trifle overcooked but the toast was just as he had promised. With her mouth full of honey and butter, it was hard to make the sweeping statement she had in mind, to declare that she would absolutely never drive him—or anyone else—anywhere when he was drunk. He was gazing out of the small kitchen window. A tea strainer hung from a nail over a pane and he seemed to be squinting through it, as though to see the world differently.

She wanted to know what he was thinking about. She had never been especially interested in what adults were thinking until this moment of studying her father's profile—unless she'd been trying to out-guess or outwit them.

People claimed they spoke about their thoughts, their feelings. She had often wondered if another kind of conversation was taking place, wordlessly, at the same time. No matter what you talked about with Harriet Blacking, she was really saying—*you can't fool me*—and you were always protesting—*I'm not trying to fool you!* Her conversations with Cornelia were partly about how much they liked each other. When she asked Cornelia if she could borrow a blouse and Cornelia said yes, but don't get strawberry jam on it, they were both saying—you can have what is mine. And when she and Philippe talked in the café where she sometimes met him after his Thursday anthropology class, whatever they said, it was about being glad to see each other—there wasn't anyone they wanted to see more, even if they argued about drinking coffee black or with milk, or when Philippe was going to stop smoking, or why the Conservatives were so boring. Their words were paper boats float-ing on a river—a strong current of delight and ex-citement that was the other, hidden conversation between them.

"I'm thinking about you," Catherine's father said. "And what a nice girl you are."

She was startled. She had an impulse to thank

him for being plain, for not making a joke. She didn't. He might think she was criticizing him.

She would like very much to tell him that often his jokes tired her out, even though she laughed, and that the joking made her feel as if a door were being pushed shut against her. Was there another conversation, she wondered, going on between the two of them, too? Beneath all the jokes?

The back door opened and shut. It would be Mrs. Landy. Mr. Ames had gotten her name from the Mackenzie postmistress.

"Postmistresses know everything worth knowing," Mr. Ames had told Catherine. "Don't forget that."

Mrs. Landy was making mouse noises in the hall. She would be hanging up the jacket she always wore, no matter how warm the day. In a moment she appeared at the kitchen door, thin as a hairpin, with hairpin legs and a little twist of mouse hair on the top of her head.

"Dear Mrs. Landy," said Mr. Ames. "I'm glad to see you!"

"I was just here yesterday," Mrs. Landy said.

"And here you are again today!" exclaimed Mr. Ames. "Is everything fine at home? How is Jackie?"

"My little Jackie is just fine," said Mrs. Landy, in her faintly mournful voice. "But Mr. Conklin, the bus driver, nearly wrecked the bus this morning with us all in it, he was driving so crazy. A good thing the road isn't much traveled."

Catherine glanced at her father. He gave her a conspiratorial wink. She didn't smile; it wasn't funny.

"We'll leave you to your labors," Mr. Ames said.

Mrs. Landy tittered. "The way you talk, Mr. Ames," she said.

Catherine followed him outdoors. He looked up at the sky and spread wide his arms as though to embrace it. The early fog had cleared away, the sky was cloudless, the July sun, brilliant.

She still hadn't said what she wanted to say about last night. It was like a lump in her throat. She had shaved him. They had had breakfast. They had had conversations. It was a summer day and everything was fine.

Was it fine? She felt again the fear and disgust she had felt last night on that wild country road; she heard again those groans and snores from the back seat.

"I don't want to do that again," she said in a low, steady voice. He bent to listen to her. "Like last night," she said.

"I know," he responded gravely. "I know just how bad it was. For you and for me. It won't happen again. And now it's time you learned to shoot." He went back inside the house.

She knew he had gone to fetch the rifle he'd found wrapped up in newspapers in a closet and which she'd watched him clean the first day of her visit.

She was immensely relieved that she had spoken about last night, not that she entirely believed what he'd said—that it wouldn't happen again. And along with the relief, she felt that stirring of anticipation he was always able to arouse in her.

He had done that from the earliest times she could recall seeing him, even when he was only taking her to have a hamburger in some bar where he could order German beer. He would show her the label, point out how beautiful it was, and then tell her everything about it, how the beer was made, what the city was like where it came from, the feel of it, the cold, stinging, hearty, blessed rush of it down one's parched throat. He'd given her a spoonful once, and when she'd made a face, finding it bitter, he'd laughed.

"It doesn't taste the way you said it would," she'd said to him reproachfully.

"Ah, you're learning to be a critic," he'd replied.

❧❧ ❧❧ ❧❧ ❧❧ ❧❧ ❧❧ Three

A TRAIN used to pass once a day through the back-yard on its way to Lunenberg, Mrs. Landy told the Ameses. Catherine pressed aside thick clumps of grass with her foot and bent to touch the rusted track. What had happened to the passengers who had traveled on that one-car train to the fishing town on the Atlantic Ocean? Who had lived in the little house in those days? Mr. Ames didn't know the house's history, but he offered to provide Catherine with one, or several, if she liked.

"I want the real one," she said.

"It wouldn't be more interesting than what I could invent. Less so, probably," he'd responded.

She wandered around to the back of the house where there was a narrow porch but no door. Perhaps the original owners had been afraid they'd tumble out and over the edge of a low cliff a few yards away. Beyond the cliff lay a broad meadow, its farthest border a meandering stream. A few miles beyond the stream was the village of Mackenzie.

When he arrived there, Mr. Ames said he knew he had come to the right place. "I'm an old hand at finding good places," he'd told her. "It's because I know what I'm after. Do you know a village has temperament and character just as a person has? I saw that it was rural here without being brutal."

She imagined him parking the big car the morning he'd driven down Mackenzie's main street, talking to people in his easy, confiding way, which, she guessed, flattered them and made them want to trust him and do things for him. There was a pub in the village; he'd probably gone there in the evening and met Mr. Conklin and Farmer Glimm.

He had lived in so many places in Europe and in the United States, too, all along the eastern coast, Key West, towns along the Chesapeake, all over New England. "I'm settling down at last," he would write her. The rest of the letter would be a description of the village or town, the beach, the headland, the bay, so detailed it was as though he was making a map.

After he had married Emma, Catherine's mother had wondered if he would indeed settle down at last, but the return addresses on envelopes continued to change every year or so.

She heard him calling her and she rounded the house and found him standing near the tracks, holding the rifle at his side. She hadn't been sure he had seriously meant to teach her to shoot even after he'd bought ammunition in Mackenzie. He had often said they were going to do one thing but changed his mind because he'd thought of something more interesting.

He'd had a gun collection when he lived on Cape Cod. An arsonist had burned down his house and everything in it had been destroyed. That was when he was young, before he'd met and married Catherine's mother. She gave Catherine a photograph of him in his little saltbox house near Pilgrim Lake, sitting in front of a wicker table, a portable typewriter on it as well as a cat curled up next to an ashtray. In the picture, he looked so thin, staring down at the typewriter, writing his first novel.

She didn't care about learning to shoot. What she wanted was to get him talking about his early times. Why had he always sought out the sea? Where had he gotten the money to rent that house and buy guns and live and eat? And what about his parents? Her grandparents? Where had they come from? All that she knew about his early history was that he'd been born in New York City.

She didn't know ordinary things about him, things the other Dalraida students knew about their fathers and took for granted—how they behaved with their families in their homes, what they thought about politics and art and the way the world was going, what work they did. What she did know about him was how he felt about what he read, the delight in his face when he mentioned certain poets, how he saw the comic side of familiar things most people never noticed, how he never took anything at all for granted. And, she thought ruefully, how many other of the students had seen their father passed out cold in the back seat of a car?

"What's that look mean?" he asked her intently.

She didn't want to tell him what was in her mind.

"I was thinking about the farmer's wife," she answered, pretty sure he wouldn't care to follow that line of discussion. He ran his hand along the stock of the gun. Then he looked up at her. "What's that you're wearing? What's the *North Face*?"

Catherine looked down at her T-shirt. "I guess it's the north face of some mountain."

He shook his head. "Don't be a sheep, Cath," he said. "Don't follow fashion."

"I have one with Virginia Woolf's face on it," she said defensively.

"Worse yet," he said. "Nobody reads her work, just gossip about her. Why don't you wear one with a snapshot of God?"

"I have read Virginia Woolf," Catherine replied sharply. "I read *Orlando*."

He walked on, crossing the tracks and setting off down a narrow dirt road opposite to the blacktop they took to Mackenzie. "You ought, at least, to know the name of that mountain," he said over his shoulder.

"I'll make up a mountain," she said, following him. "The way you were going to make up a story about who owned our house."

He laughed then. "Philadelphia lawyer," he said.

The road soon led them among low hills on whose long slopes spruce trees stood, motionless and solemn looking. They trudged along through the warm, silent landscape. Catherine grew drowsy; the few hours of sleep on the horsehair sofa hadn't done her much good. A sudden liquid rise and fall of bird song startled her. She caught up with him and glanced at his face. He was pale. His shoulders were stiff, as though he were carrying too heavy a burden. She knew he wasn't feeling well. She started to ask him if he knew what kind of bird had sung, but she didn't.

She didn't want conversation at that moment. It was a chance to study him and think about him. It was just such a moment of private observation that made this time with him so different.

When he talked, when he gestured with his hands and arms, she thought she'd never seen anyone so tenanted with emotion, ideas. They had not been able to afford silence until now. When they met for their visits there had been so much to tell, to ask.

Last spring, he had brought Emma along to their visit for the first time, though they'd already been married two years. Catherine had seen how gone Emma was on him. She'd not taken her eyes from his face except when Catherine spilled her ginger ale on the restaurant table. She glanced at Catherine then as though she were a shadow in a dream she was having. She hadn't been unpleasant. She'd even tried to show interest in the usual things—Catherine's school and what she liked about it, or didn't like, what movies she went to, what she wanted to be when she grew up.

Catherine had noted how expensive her clothes looked, how intricate and beautiful the three rings she wore. One was a large diamond on her wedding-ring finger that Catherine guessed Emma had given herself. She was sure her father couldn't have afforded such a ring. There had always been the tug of money between him and her mother. She'd heard about that, of course. If your parents were divorced, you always heard about money. Sometimes he was so late with support checks, they would turn to Granny, her mother's mother, who lived a meticulous life like a fine old clock ticking silently, in a stone house in New Hope, Pennsylvania; a house full of antiques people were always trying to persuade her to sell.

She would give them money and she would always remark how much she had liked Harry Ames. In her cool, remote voice, she would observe that he was a bundle of trouble but worth it, though it might not be for her to say. "Then don't," Catherine recalled her mother saying. She remembered, too, the flush that had spread over Granny's fine, pale skin.

When Catherine described Emma to her mother, the clothes, the rings, she'd commented somewhat grimly, "He found someone to take care of him. Not many of us can afford the luxury of a husband who wrote two novels before he was twenty-six and hasn't managed to write his daughter a decent, fatherly letter since she was born."

There were things, Catherine had begun to understand, that were so untrue there was no point in arguing about them. When Mr. Ames telephoned Catherine from Athens on her twelfth birthday, her mother had said, "He'd rather spend thirty dollars than buy a stamp. He'd never look up a phone number in the telephone book the way normal people do—always got the operator to do it for him and considered himself a sport for it."

Normal. Decent. Catherine kicked up the dust. Like Carter, she supposed her mother meant. Carter was as calm as a sofa. A normal sofa. Her father actually did make a living writing travel books, mostly about Scandinavia. She'd asked him why he didn't live in Oslo or Uppsala, or one of those places he wrote about. He had answered that he detested the whole northern world. Catherine had laughed at the extravagance of what he said. He went straight to Italy whenever he could afford it, he told her, and he had vowed never to write a guide for use in that country. He didn't want to encourage still more tourists to go there.

"Let's pause a minute," he said. "My character may be better than yours but my legs aren't."

He grinned at her and went to a straggly oak by the side of the road and leaned against its trunk. Catherine squatted down and watched an ant dragging a dead beetle, twice its size, around a small stone.

"How's my old wife?" he asked. It was the first time he'd asked about Catherine's mother.

"She's not so old," Catherine replied. "And she's fine."

"Still slaving away for that swine of a publisher?"

"She's the chief copy editor now," Catherine said. "The man she works for is very nice."

"Very nice," he repeated. "What does that mean? Chocolate pudding and a song at twilight are very nice."

Catherine stood up and walked rapidly away from him, down the road. He called after her, "Don't get sore! Though it does you credit."

"I'm not sore," she called back. "It's just so boring!"

It wasn't boring. It was confusing and unsettling. She wanted to hear more, though she was afraid of what he might tell her. It was like a door slowly opening in a suspense movie. Would something frightful walk through that door? At best, her mother spoke of him as though he were a naughty child she had had to put up with, and he spoke about her as though everything she did were touched with foolishness.

She imagined the two of them jeering and sneering at each other as they walked down the aisle to be married. But it couldn't have been like that!

He caught up with her and placed his hand flat on her head. " 'Jane, Jane, tall as a crane,' " he murmured. It was his quoting voice. She didn't ask him, as she usually did, whom he was quoting.

"Don't tell me I'll understand everything so much better when I'm older," she said resentfully.

"I? Tell you such a stupid thing?" He grabbed her hair and held it straight up. She stood there like a cat held by the scruff of its neck. "I'll never tell you that," he said. "I understand life less and less. My certainties lie dead, strewn over the battlefields of the past."

"You're boasting!" she cried.

He laughed and let go of her hair. "You think you're pretty smart, don't you!" he said. She heard pride and pleasure in his voice and knew it was about her. He'd liked what she said. She couldn't help but smile. He took hold of her arm for a moment, then let go of it.

"Your mother was a sweet girl," he said. "I have nothing against her. She couldn't stand my ways. She's a daylight woman."

They walked half a mile or so in silence. She was thinking hard about what he said—how he sounded superior to his own marriage, his past, as though he'd believed all along what he believed now.

The heat, the blueness of the air, the insect whirr, the scents of evergreen trees and dust simmered gently, a summer stew. He had been speaking for a while before she realized it. She'd been set to dreaming by the quiet and the warmth, and her own thoughts, which had trailed off like vapor trails in the sky.

"—intensity of hope, of feeling," he was saying. "I wonder if there is ever such a mix of giddiness and seriousness in anything as there is in love. Perhaps in revolution. Love is revolutionary . . . you'll see. Oh, you'll see how love is! Of course, you were right in your instinct to resent my condescension toward Beatrice. I don't really feel about her that way."

Beatrice . . . her mother's name. *Beatrice*, who had existed long before *Mom*.

"I'll tell you what Hawthorne said: 'When a real and strong affection has come to an end, it is not well to mock the sacred with a show of those commonplace civilities that belong to ordinary intercourse.' Do you understand that?"

She felt oppressed—all those wise sayings. She didn't want to be his student.

"I got a fortune cookie message once. It said: 'Your true love is a gunboat,' " she said, feeling that she'd like to do a little jeering herself.

"My girl, you'll have to put up with parental advice and quotes and warnings. Then you can throw it away and learn your own truths. In time, you'll bore and oppress your own children with them."

"I won't oppress my own children."

"Oho! The hell you won't!" he said boisterously.

The hills around them were higher now. A crumbling stone wall held back a sea of wildflowers. From a single rafter of a shed a fan of weathered slats hung down toward the ground. On a crest, an old barn stood like a sentry. Despite the signs of human activity, the hills looked deserted, empty of human life. Mr. Ames stepped forward, raised the rifle, and took aim at the barn. A second later, Catherine heard glass shattering.

"You shot out a window!"

"Don't worry!" he said, so quickly his words seemed part of the reverberation of the shot. "I've looked into it. Those are abandoned buildings. Come here. I want to show you how to stand when you fire a rifle."

There were many things to do at the same time. place her feet correctly, learn to sight through the tiny antler at the end of the long barrel, fit the stock in the right place on her shoulder.

"Go ahead," he ordered. "Shoot before you start to worry."

Catherine aimed at the shed, which already looked as if it were about to stumble down the slope and collapse in a heap on the road. She pulled the trigger and shouted, "No!" at the same time. Through the sound of the shot, she heard her father laughing.

"Well—you *can* hit the side of a shed," he said. "And you mustn't shout *no*. The bullet might turn around and hit your dear papa."

She was dazed but exuberant, and she wanted to try again at once. Mr. Ames said it was best to scatter their shots and not concentrate them in one place— in case.

"In case—what?" she demanded.

"I suppose people own these derelicts even though they aren't used. I suppose Canadians have the same property obsession as our own countrymen."

They went on past thickets of raspberry mixed in with small dense stands of oak and high wild tangles of lacelike shrubbery. The meadows hummed with insect life. The road itself began to fade away, as though the underbush was slowly erasing it. There were no more buildings to shoot at, so Catherine shot at branches her father would point to. Once, by error, she hit a utility pole.

"How's that school? I liked that grand old dame, Madame Soul," he said, after they had used up the ammunition.

"Madame Soule," she corrected him. "Some of the girls think she's pretty crazy. But I like her, too. She worries about the state of the world."

"Quite right. So she should. And there's a villain, isn't there? There's always a villain at work in any community, like the snake in Eden."

Was there anything she could tell him that would surprise him?

"Well . . . yes."

"Tell me about her."

"Harriet Blacking. She sneers," Catherine said.

"Sneer back—in your own fashion."

"You always feel she knows something terrible about you," Catherine said.

"That's why villains are so successful," he said. "Because they do know something—our secret villainies we try to hide from ourselves. They feed on secrets like termites feeding on wood—and bring the house down—only because we try to defend ourselves against our own charges. My advice to you is—admit you're a villain and attack!"

He was walking a few steps ahead of her, his head down, the rifle held loosely in one hand as he gestured with the other. He was speaking to himself, she suspected.

"They get the goods on us," he said.

Moved by an impulse of pity she couldn't explain to herself, Catherine caught up with him and took his arm. For a second, she rested her head against his shoulder.

"Thanks, pal," he said. "Thanks for that."

When they reached the house, they found Mrs. Landy about to have lunch in the kitchen. They'd discovered at once, when they sat down to the first meal she had prepared for them, that she was a frightful cook, frying meat as though she were trying to tan it, and adding a jelly glass of milk, but no butter, to two boiled potatoes that she had mashed with a tablespoon.

Mr. Ames hoped to discourage her cooking, without hurting her feelings, by fixing her lunch himself. Today he had left her an immense sandwich of spinach, sardines, hard-boiled egg, and slices of onion.

Mrs. Landy turned to them, holding the sandwich in her knobby little hands, an expression of amazement on her face. "I never saw such a thing, Mr. Ames," she said. "It looks like a picture in a magazine. Dare I eat it?"

"We are here to administer first aid," said Mr. Ames. "Go ahead, Mrs. Landy. Take heart. Take a bite."

"I can see you two been having fun," she said, in her rather mournful way.

Mr. Ames put his arm around her and hugged her. "Mrs. Landy, you're sharp as a tack—as we said in the days of my youth."

Mrs. Landy giggled and shook her head. "You are a funny man," she said. "I tell my little Jackie all the things you say as best as I can remember them. I'm going to take this sandwich home and show it to him."

She wrapped up the sandwich carefully and put it in a paper bag. Mr. Ames walked her to the door. She would go across the tracks to the tarmac road and catch the bus, driven by Mr. Conklin. Catherine heard her father telling Mrs. Landy how sweet she made the little house look, how lovely the Canadian summer was—as though there weren't summer everywhere. She ran to the parlor window to watch them. Her father still had his arm around Mrs. Landy

He seemed about to lead her into a dance to music she had never heard.

When he returned, Catherine was standing in the hall. He didn't seem to know she was there. He held up one hand and bit his thumb, then he saw her. He simply stood, letting her look at him, at his somber, elderly face. She didn't know she had reached out her hand as though to prevent him from falling until he walked past her. Had she offended him?

He didn't offer to make her lunch. He watched her as she ate a piece of bread and cheese and drank cold coffee from a glass. His skin was ashen. Mrs. Landy's dance was over, the music stopped. His face was like a room where the only light had been turned off. She had not seen him like this. When he spoke at last, his voice was so low she had to lean toward him to hear his words.

"I feel terrible . . . things catching up. A nap will put it right. You must be tired, too. Let's call it a day for a little while." He left the kitchen. She could hear his slow steps on the stairs.

She went to her own room and drew down the thin canvas shade over the window. For a few minutes, she tried to read Daudet's *Lettres de mon moulin*. Gratefully, she felt sleep begin to cover her like a blanket lightly drawn up.

When Catherine awoke it was twilight. She heard her father moving around the kitchen. She washed her face and combed her hair and went downstairs. He came out into the hall to greet her.

"I'm myself. I'm better. I've recovered," he said, smiling. He carried two glasses. "Soda and a bit of lemon for both of us," he said.

Where had the sick, elderly man gone whom she'd seen in the hall hours earlier?

"Shall we take a stroll on the deck?" he asked. She followed him outside and to the antique swing that stood a few yards from the porch. It was built of wooden slats; the two seats faced each other. Beneath them was a floor like a duckboard. When Catherine and Mr. Ames sat down in the swing, it gave out pleasant wood squeaks, the only sound except for the faint hushing of swallows' wings as the birds rose and fell in the fading light. The lengthening shadows of the trees that bordered the shallow stream lay upon the meadow grass like a ghostly snow fence.

"It's the best time of day," he said. "Look—there's a cat way down there near that willow."

The cat was crouched on a mound of earth beneath the tree.

"What is it thinking about?" Catherine wondered.

"Supper and escape," he replied. "Like the rest of us."

She laughed.

He said, "No riotous behavior, please. Tell me what you really like best about school."

"When we go to the ski cabin in the mountains. The train is always filled with people. They walk up and down the aisle laughing and talking. They wear bright sweaters and caps and they shout because they're happy about where they're going. Skis stick out everywhere like pins in a pincushion. When we arrive, it's night. It's a little train, maybe like the one that used to go through the backyard here. The station in the mountains is tiny, just a shed. We get out and crunch on the snow in our ski boots. The train starts back to Montreal. It's really dark. You can just barely make out the shapes of people as they go off to wherever they're going. Enormous horse-drawn sledges are waiting for everyone. We take two of them. The drivers are muffled up in moth-eaten fur rugs—there are rugs for us, too. The horses begin to climb up the road, which runs along the mountainside. You can look across the valley and see small lights on those other slopes. Your hands are warm beneath the rug but your face is nearly frozen, and the air is so crisp you feel you could break off pieces of it like mica. And it has a wonderful smell—you keep sniffing it, breathing it in, trying to catch hold of it. If the moon is out, or the stars, you can see the whole long valley. Oh—it's so mysterious, so beautiful! And everything about the horses is beautiful, their smell, their great legs pulling, pulling. And the snow is everywhere, like a different world. . . ."

"Snow," he said reflectively. "It's like twilight when all the hurry and noise of things stops."

The swing squeaked; the swallows dipped and rose like fish in a clear stream. She told him about the time she and Cornelia got hold of a gallon of red wine made by people who lived in a small village in those mountains. They had drunk all of it, sitting in a bunk while the other girls were out skiing. Madame had called her downstairs to discuss the United Nations and what was wrong with that organization, and she, Catherine, had to hang onto the back of a chair for dear life so as not to fall flat on her face. She and Cornelia had been sick for three days, throwing up, dizzy and shaken. How that bunk had flown around the room! And they so weak they could only wait for it to settle so they could lie down and groan.

"Now that you've done that once, you don't have to do it again," he said neutrally. With a touch of sternness, he added, "Don't do it again, Catherine. It's a fool's way."

"I know," she said.

They were silent for a long time. The sky welled up with night. At last, he sighed and said, "Suppertime." They walked back to the house, their arms linked.

He made their supper while she sat on the horsehair sofa and looked though old issues of the Canadian edition of *Time* magazine. He had concocted a dessert he called no-name pudding, in honor of an Italian called D'Annunzio who had, himself, invented a dessert, *senzanome*—without a name, he told her.

Catherine didn't always listen closely to her father. She listened, as it were, at a distance, catching a phrase or a name, the way she listened to music. He didn't seem to mind. He never asked her, as other grown-ups did—Are you listening to me? Did you hear what I said? Are you daydreaming?

He used up every pot and pan in the kitchen and it took them quite some time to clean up.

"It drove your mother mad," he said, "the way I made such a mess in the kitchen. I don't like it to be neat—it would affect my cooking. Neat cooking is extremely repulsive and ungenerous, and it worries too much about the future."

"Neat cooks can turn out a good meal, too, just as good as one of yours," she declared. She knew she was defending her mother, who was so tidy in the kitchen it hardly seemed possible she had cooked a meal.

He shot her a knowing look. "No, they can't," he said. "And you know it!"

He was going to read to her, he told her. It would settle her digestion. Her digestion was fine, she protested, a protest left over, she knew, from his pronouncement about the right way to cook. He interrupted her with falsetto screams, a look of mischief on his face, screeching, "No! No! My tumtum is perfect!" pretending it was she speaking. She laughed helplessly. It was what being disarmed meant, she guessed.

He had brought with him an Evelyn Waugh anthology. Slumping into the armchair in the parlor, he announced he was going to read her a story called "A Handful of Dust."

At moments, it was difficult to follow the story because she was watching his expressive face, listening to the sound of his voice. It was resonant, sometimes as mournful and deep as a church bell. He was like an actor, she thought, then, no, he wasn't like an actor. He was reading only for himself.

He looked up from time to time but not at her. He held out his hand in a gesture of emphasis as though he read words he'd written.

It had been the longest day of her life, she told herself when she lay down at last on the narrow bed in her room under the eaves. It was a day that started dreadfully and ended happily. Living with her father was like living with a crowd of people. One of that crowd was a drunken man, a smudged outline of a person with a voice as soggy as a wet sponge.

She tried to recall all that he had said that day, all that they had seen and done, as though to fix everything in a scrapbook of remembrance, as though even the time she was still to spend with him was already in the past.

But now as sleep began to overtake her, the only moment she could clearly recall was when they had opened the door to the house. He had looked back at the sky, flaring with darkness and the last rays of the sun, and said so softly she barely heard him . . . "the romance of life."

Four

THIS WAS the surprise: to wake to her father's voice; to see him standing in the doorway. He was telling her that he was off to Mackenzie to persuade Reverend Ross to go fishing with them today. "Go back to sleep," he said. She was slept out.

If she had been used to him, would she have been so aware of his living presence? Perhaps you didn't think about ordinary, familiar things until you lost them. Lying in her bed, feeling the pleasant coolness of the morning air, she thought about thought itself.

"Think!" Madame Soule exhorted the Dalraida students. No one told you how to do it. And, she told herself, it didn't have to stop you from having breakfast.

She dressed, took the steps two at a time, and raced into the kitchen, suddenly happy to have the house to herself. Because they had no telephone, Mr. Ames would drive right to the Reverend Ross's parsonage. He'd met him before Catherine had arrived in Nova Scotia. In the post office, he'd told her, the second important social center of the village. The pub, of course, was the first. Mr. Ames had discovered that the minister was wild about fishing and knew all the best spots in the countryside. He was hoping he could prevail upon him to guide them to a trout stream he had mentioned, about twenty-five miles north of Mackenzie. Catherine cleaned the last of her fried egg from her plate with a piece of bread. She didn't doubt that her father would prevail.

She heard the car return and ran to the parlor window. Mr. Ames took several paper sacks from the back seat and put them on the ground. He looked up at the sky, lit a cigarette, crossed his arms, and leaned against the car. She didn't know whether his eyes were closed because of the cigarette smoke, or because he was exhausted by his early-morning effort. And all for her entertainment, she thought uneasily. She realized he was now looking straight at her. He waved, stamped out the cigarette, and grabbed up the sacks. She went to meet him at the door.

"We don't have to do things all the time," she said. "I like hanging around, just reading or something."

"Or something," he repeated mockingly. "Now cut that out! This isn't a generosity contest. I'm doing everything for myself alone. And for God's sake, find a better word than *something*! The Reverend is delighted to let us in on his secret place— and not for godly reasons, either. I'd better warn you, he's a ferocious prig. He'd have me in chains if he heard a word about our adventure the other night with poor old Farmer Glimm and Mr. Conklin."

"He probably has," she said. He certainly had no reason to speak so patronizingly about those two men.

"No one ever tells ministers anything," he replied. "For fear of offending their delicate sensibilities. Anyhow, you don't have to convince the church of human weakness."

They made a picnic lunch and put it in an old straw hamper she'd found in a closet.

"I always want to eat a picnic the minute it's made," she said.

"Me, too," he said companionably. "In fact, once I did. It was when I first knew your mother. We made a marvelous picnic—we had planned to go to some New Jersey beach, I think, but instead, we sat down on a Navajo rug in the living room and ate it all up."

"What living room?" she asked. "What Navajo rug?"

He looked at her pensively. "Of course, you would like to know all of it, wouldn't you? I think we bought that rug in Taos—"

"—I didn't know you and Mom had been there."

"Oh, we wandered quite a lot. There was life before you, Cath."

"I know that."

"I guess you do. And the living room . . . that was probably Cape May. I remember so much I wish I didn't. But I forget the sequence of events and the places where we lived. Another thing Beatrice couldn't bear in the long run—all that moving about. Tidal drifting, she called it."

Catherine went upstairs to get a sweater. He said she might need it later in the day. When she returned, she found him still in the kitchen. He held a drink of whiskey in his hand. The bottle was open on the counter. He looked at her defiantly.

"A small one," he said. "There's a certain strain being around the Reverend."

He brought the glass to his lips, then swallowed its contents in one gulp, his throat working convulsively. He put the glass in the sink and grinned at her. "There. That's better. Now we'll go pick him up at the parsonage. Let's go. It's a longish drive to that stream. You'd better stuff your ears with cotton. He's a nonstop talker."

She said nothing. He looked at her questioningly. The silence between them grew dense with words not said. Catherine stared at the open bottle.

"Don't ride me, Catherine," he muttered. "I won't be told what to do"—his voice rose suddenly—"especially not by young females!"

She turned on her heel and went out of the kitchen, out of the house, and got into the car. Two fishing rods lay on the back seat. A bluebottle fly buzzed against the windshield. She realized she was afraid. How violently he had thrown the whiskey down his throat! How he shuddered as though it hurt him! Oh, the fly was so stupid! "Here!" she cried, trying to steer it with her hand toward the open window. "Can't you speak English?" It swerved out, then flew back into the car. "There's no saving you," she said to it.

She had driven those drunken men home in the dramatic middle of the night. She had thought it was all over the next morning. At least, she had hoped it was. Finding her father in the kitchen just now, the sunlight falling on the counter, her breakfast plates draining in the small dish rack, she had felt the depth of her ignorance. She only knew that there was danger.

He was coming toward the car from the house, walking briskly, rubbing his hands as though he were chilled. He got into the car and bent forward to start it, saying, "Ah . . ." when the motor turned over. "*Va t'en*," he said, brushing at the fly, which flew away for good this time. A French-speaking fly, she thought.

Her father did so many things easily, but he drove as though he were pursued by devils—jaw clenched, eyes peering ahead as if a thick fog had formed, a permanent one, in front of the windshield. Had he taken a second drink, or a third?

She felt him glance over at her.

"It'll be a good day," he promised. "You'll see."

She thought of how she and the other Dalraida students tried to outdo each other describing the monstrous amounts of liquor Madame LeSueur was supposed to consume, how they imitated her walking up the stairs with her mad, precarious dignity. She recollected how sick she and Cornelia had been on that mountain wine. How could anyone want to feel so horrible?

"Do you like your new stepfather?" Mr. Ames asked.

His question took her by surprise. With an emphasis that startled her, she answered. "Yes. Very much." Did she? She was about to say that Carter was nice. She didn't want her father to ask her what *that* meant.

"A steady sort of chap?" he asked lightly.

"Steady? I don't know about that," Catherine replied. "He's kind."

"Kind. Kind to kittens and tots? And steady, I'm sure. And certain. Oh, to be certain," he said.

They didn't speak again until he had parked in front of Reverend Ross's parsonage.

"It's doubt that makes one think," he said then. "Certainty answers everything."

She wanted to argue with him, but before she could speak, she saw an elderly man walking down a path toward them. She didn't, in any case, know what she would have said.

"How do you do," the Reverend said to her with a nod as he got into the car. He had a weatherbeaten face and a large jaw. She had started to give him her seat in the front. He shook his head vigorously. "No, no," he said in a deep, baying voice. While they drove the narrow country road to the trout stream—the Reverend's secret place—he told them what Catherine suspected was the entire history, with footnotes, of the Maritime Provinces.

Mr. Ames parked the car in a field. The three of them climbed a low stone wall and walked through a meadow, where the grass grew as high as their waists, down the slope to a line of willow trees. The secret place was a wide, shallow stream strewn with boulders, sonorous with the sound of rushing water.

The Reverend held a finger to his lips. "Not a word," he whispered, "or they'll hear us." He waded out into the stream in his high rubber boots. Like an important conductor about to lead an important symphony orchestra, he raised high his fishing rod.

"Do you think he'll stop for our picnic?" Catherine asked her father.

"Patience, child," he replied in a low voice. "Eat a few leaves, a twig or two. Be dignified. Don't howl for your dinner. Here. Stand here . . . I want you to learn how to use this thing."

But she couldn't get the hang of casting. Her line caught in the branches of a willow. It flew everywhere except behind the rock her father pointed to.

She glimpsed a brown fish lurking a few yards away just beneath the surface of the water. "Why don't I just pick it up?" she asked.

Her father snorted with laughter, looking somewhat nervously to where the minister stood casting effortlessly. "You just try! They're cunning creatures. I fear you're no match for them."

She was relieved when he went off by himself, as the Reverend had done. It was agreeable to sit on the bank and watch the two men, so still except for the graceful motions of their arms as they cast, reeled in, cast again and again. The water flashed where sunlight touched it. She heard the delicate buzzing of the reels as the lines flew out, arced, rested lightly, briefly, on the surface of the stream.

Her father appeared to be as absorbed as the Reverend. Was it because he glanced over at her from time to time that she felt he was giving a performance of a man fishing? Not only for her but for himself? She dozed a while, read *A Child's Christmas in Wales*, which she nearly knew by heart, then went for a walk through the meadow back to the stone wall, following it for half a mile or so until it dwindled to a few moss-covered rocks near the lip of a small pit. In the pit, she saw the skeleton of what had been a little animal. She squatted down and stared at it. She could have touched the clean, bleached bones that formed the rib cage. The heat of the sunlight on her back had weight like a full pack. The sudden drumming of a woodpecker was loud, a door rapped with a cane. She stood abruptly and turned away from the pit. With long strides, she followed the wall back to the point where she had begun to follow it. She was frightened, though she could not think why she should be. When she reached the willow trees and saw the two men standing beneath them on the stream's bank, she felt comforted, as she did when she awoke from a bad dream and knew it to be only that.

Mr. Ames was admiring the Reverend's four trout. He had had no luck himself.

"You must take three of them," the Reverend said, adding that he and his wife ate only light, modest suppers.

Mr. Ames said crankily to Catherine, "Look. You've left your Dylan Thomas on the ground. That's no way to treat a book."

She took it from his hand and put it in a back pocket of her jeans. She supposed he was cross because he hadn't caught anything. She quickly spread out the picnic on a blanket she had taken from her bed. She noticed how suspiciously the Reverend was regarding the food, the deviled eggs and ham and tomato sandwiches, the thick wedge of cheddar, a box of cupcakes, this last which Catherine had asked for despite her father's scornful remark about mass-produced food.

Reverend Ross picked up a deviled egg and stared at it closely. A modest supper made you rest easy at night, he declared. And a modest lunch left your mind clear for reflection. He had several theories about the way people ate, he said. There were those who snapped at their food like foxes. Others mooned over their dinners and made designs with their forks in mashed potatoes. In church, he had observed that the snappers threw down communion wine as though it were rum, but the mooners and dreamers sipped it like fine wine. Each type, he said, consumed the Lord in his own way.

Mr. Ames looked very patient. He was holding a sandwich and staring at the egg the Reverend continued to hold on his outstretched palm. "I think, after all, I'll just have a bit of that cheese," Ross said at last.

"I admire your restraint," Mr. Ames said.

"It is not restraint. It's fear of indigestion," the Reverend answered coolly.

Her father stuffed the sandwich in his mouth. The Reverend continued his sermon on feeding habits, taking bits of cheese from time to time. When Mr. Ames offered him coffee from a Thermos, he observed, "Coffee is not good for us." Mr. Ames then lit a cigarette. Reverend Ross shook his head and rolled his eyes at the heavens, then walked to the edge of the stream, turning his back on Catherine and her father. But Mr. Ames followed him and clumsily, Catherine observed, intruded himself between the minister and the water. In a rush of words, Catherine heard him praising Ross for his casting technique. He was stammering. Why was he grinning so doggishly?

"Time we were going back, Mr. Ames, don't you think?" the Reverend asked.

Humbly, it seemed to Catherine, her father helped her gather up the picnic things and load the car. He even slid humbly into the driver's seat. It must have been the Reverend who had managed to bring about all this meekness in her father, but Catherine couldn't figure out how he'd done it—unless it was by his apparent disapproval of everything. He hadn't spoken to her at all. Perhaps he thought of her as a divorced child and not worthy of conversation. Yet when they dropped him off at his parsonage, carrying his one fish for his modest supper, he said rather sternly that he had had a splendid time. They must do it again. "Perhaps the girl will learn to cast—if she's given proper instruction."

"That was pretty funny," Mr. Ames remarked, as they drove on toward home. "I don't think the old horse even knew you were there—or me, either, for that matter. He certainly doesn't exude the warmth of Christian love, does he? Heavens! I couldn't get his attention for one minute."

That was it, Catherine realized. It was what had made her father so uneasy. The Reverend had been indifferent to him, had treated him as if he were just anybody. But who was *anybody*? Why should *anybody* be treated with indifference? She hadn't liked the Reverend; he seemed a tight, rough man. Yet she felt faintly shamed by Mr. Ames's efforts to charm him. Why on earth did he want to charm him?

"Even parsons have secret thoughts," he remarked to her later that evening, as they sat in the swing on the edge of the cliff. "Even they divide the world into opposing groups. I must say I prefer good and bad to Ross's division between gulpers and sippers. What a vision of human character!"

"You divide the world in half. My mother on one side, you on the other."

He looked perplexed.

"You called her a daylight person," she reminded him. "Are you a moonlight person?"

"You store away everything, don't you? If I said

that, it was foolish. After all, there are only men and women. As for being a moonlight person, the truth is I've lived most of my life in a dense fog."

"Why didn't you ever have me to visit you and Emma?" she asked abruptly.

Mr. Ames put his foot on the ground to stop the slight motion of the swing. They hung there, motionless, for what seemed a very long time, as darkness deepened around them. At last he spoke quietly, sadly.

"I didn't think it would be good for you. I didn't think *I* was good for you. It was Emma who persuaded me—to try. She said—if you never got a close look at me, you'd be wondering about me all your life. I suppose you will be, anyway."

Catherine didn't care for the idea that Emma was responsible for this visit. Her father had a rather silly look on his face—thinking of Emma's wonderfulness, no doubt.

"What about what I thought?" she asked.

"That's what Emma was concerned about."

"I mean—what did *you* think about my thoughts?"

"Do I hear self-righteousness? Are you feeling badly treated? Don't—for God's sake—be a victim. It rots out the brain. You'll never have a moment of pleasure because of thinking of all the wrongs you've suffered."

She quailed at the anger she thought she heard in his voice. As though to confirm it, he got out of the swing and strode off to the house. How could he be so unfair? She followed him and at once tripped on some root or hummock. She knew it wasn't because it had grown dark. Her body had gone out of control because she'd lost inner balance.

She found him in the kitchen pouring himself a drink of whiskey.

"What about that?" she cried, a tremor in her voice. "Does that stuff keep your brain from rotting?" She remembered how his features had slackened that night of drinking, how his body had slumped. Her dismay was so great, she held out both her hands toward the bottle as though to snatch it from him. He looked at her as though she were a stranger. Her hands dropped to her sides. She felt exhausted. She felt she could go to sleep standing there next to the kitchen table.

"Don't be a prig," he said harshly. "You're old enough to know damn near everything—though not, I must add, to have any judgment. And don't tell me your sainted mother hasn't nailed me to the cross about my drinking habits."

"Mom didn't have to tell me," she said flatly. "Do you think I can't see on my own? How I hated it when you were passed out cold in the back of that horrible car!"

"Not at all," he protested. "I wasn't passed out. I was thinking."

"Do you snore and snort when you think?"

He started to laugh. He took two steps and grabbed her arms and shook her. "Cath, I won't do it again. I swear it! As for the car—if you like, we can go out and throw rocks at it!"

She didn't want him to swear to anything, to what he would or wouldn't do. "Try to understand," he urged her. She had begun to learn his face. She knew he was trying to show her how earnest and simple —and truthful—he was being. But being simple was the last thing he wanted to be. She knew that, too.

"Try to understand," he began in a conciliating voice. "I was so damned nervous about living with you. Don't you see that it's strange for both of us? Not only for you? I'm used to seeing you on the run—as though we were fugitives."

She *could* understand all that—to be nervous, to feel the strangeness of things. But was he being really truthful? What did it all have to do with his drinking?

"Oh, how hard you're thinking! I can see that poor little brain all twisted up like an acrobat."

"Don't tell me what I'm doing!" she cried out. Hadn't he heard her? He was the acrobat, or rather, a juggler, keeping a lot of objects going at the same time, plates and oranges flying through the air while he, the juggler, remained hidden behind them.

"I felt superior at first," she admitted. "Driving three idiots around in the middle of the night. It didn't last. I was afraid I'd back the car into a swamp. It kept stalling. The farmer's wife thought it was all my fault. I could tell. I was even afraid she'd set the dog on me."

"Dog?" he asked wonderingly, asking as a child might. She burst into laughter despite her indignation.

"Don't laugh at your poor old father—don't make rude fun of such a pitiful relic as I am."

"Stop that!" she shouted. "And stop laughing!"

"Me, laugh?" he asked, rolling his eyes. "A dog? My poor addled mind—have you a dog hidden away somewhere?"

She felt tears on her cheeks before she realized she was crying. She sat down at the table and held her head in her hands. She felt his hand on her hair. "I *am* sorry," he said softly. "I was only trying to amuse you and, as usual, botching things up even more. I've told you, I'll tell you again, forever if you want, that I know how hard my drunken gang was on you. Don't cry. Cath . . . look! Look at what I'm going to do. Look up!"

She raised her head.

"It's all going down the drain," he said, as he poured the remaining contents of the whiskey bottle into the sink. She heard it gurgle. She wiped her face with the back of her hand. He held up the empty bottle. Staring at it, as relieved as she was, she felt a thorn of anxiety.

You couldn't buy liquor just anywhere in Nova Scotia; you had to go to a special store run by the Liquor Control Commission. People called those stores government dairies, her father had told her. "Laws are made to be broken," he had said. "The law tells you exactly what people want to do which the law prevents them from doing. We are such a foolish sort of animal that we waste all our ingenuity finding ways around laws that protect us." That was why there was a lot of bootlegging in the area, he said. Many farmers had stills in their barns.

"I didn't mean for you to throw it all out," she said.

"Ah, feeling a touch of guilt, are you? Good! It'll make you more tractable, the way females ought to be."

He turned to the counter and began to chop an onion, then a stalk of celery. His hands worked quickly, efficiently, in a blur of movement. When he stopped, there were two small heaps of perfectly cut vegetables.

"Actually," he said, looking at her, "I have always thought women were better than men in every way."

She was sitting quietly at the table; her mind felt pale, washed like an early morning sky. "They're not better or worse," she said. "They're different. *Better* is a disguised insult."

"You astonish me," he said. He walked over to her and pushed her hair carefully behind her ears and looked down at her closely. "Nice eyes," he commented somewhat absently.

She wandered off into the living room, leaving him to his cooking. She felt tranquil. His drastic action in pouring away the whiskey had, after all, reassured her. She turned on a dinky standing lamp and sat down with a book on her lap. She had taken it from a shelf without looking at its title. She turned it over. It was *Great Expectations*. She wouldn't read; she didn't need to at this moment. She had regained the balance she had lost outside in the dark. She was content simply to sit there doing nothing.

This place might have been another planet. The silence that began with evening shadows lasted until the next morning, when she heard a car or two up on the country road, or the bus halting when Mrs.

Landy was dropped off by Mr. Conklin. Sometimes a plane passed so high overhead you could barely see it, a sliver of silver when it caught the light of the sun. It must have been as silent five hundred years ago, a thousand years ago. And there was no radio, no television set, no telephone in the house to make a person forget that immense, timeless quiet. Except for two hippies she had noticed yesterday as they were driving to Mackenzie to pick up Reverend Ross, Mackenzie itself seemed split off from modern life. And even the hippies had looked sedate, very smug as they carried their groceries in a string bag to an old panel truck upon one side of which someone had painted a swollen yellow moon. Visiting her father was like going back to another time.

He came into the living room. "I must have eggs," he announced, "and we're out of them. I saw a sign in front of a house on the Mackenzie road that said fresh eggs. Come on. Let's go get some."

"It's so late."

"If they've taken in the sign, we won't stop. Get up, Catherine. Up, up . . ."

He was full of energy now, of anticipation, as though they were setting out on an adventure. When they came to the house on the road, the headlights showed a small cardboard sign leaning against the trunk of a maple tree. It read: FRESH EGGS AND HONEY.

"I like that 'and,' " he commented. "It shows they are formal and exact."

They went up two steps to a narrow porch. There was no bell. Paint flaked on the door. A dim light glowed distantly in a window. Mr. Ames knocked. They waited for a longer time than it had taken them to drive there. When the door opened at last, they saw a large, elderly woman in a dark dress holding a kerosene lamp. A blast of warmish air smelling of vegetable soup came from inside the house. The light fell on the woman's face; it was broad, expressionless, and unlined.

"I'm sorry to disturb you at such an hour," Mr. Ames said with elaborate politeness, even bowing slightly. "I was about to make my daughter an omelet for her supper when I discovered we were out of eggs. I recalled your sign and hoped you would forgive us for stopping. Of course, if we're inconveniencing you—we're living in the Diggs house, down the—"

"I know who you are," the woman said with mysterious emphasis. "Of course I know. And it isn't inconvenient. We haven't sold any eggs today. Mother has finished her tea, and, well, do come in."

They stepped inside. From somewhere in the dark room where the light of the kerosene lamp didn't reach, there must have been a stove. Catherine felt its heat. The room was packed with chairs and tables, trunks, glass cases, two immense sofas. The woman set down her lamp on a table. If they'd just wait a minute, she'd fetch them a dozen eggs, she said, and disappeared down a hall.

Mr. Ames held up the lamp. "Look at that!" he exclaimed, pointing to a huge old-fashioned birdcage on a metal stand. In it perched a gray parrot. "Stuffed," he observed. Its glass eye gleamed in the light.

"These really are fresh," the woman said as she came back into the room.

"I hope they're not parrot eggs," whispered Mr. Ames to Catherine.

"You're looking at our Tweedy," the woman said with a certain warmth. "He was our darling. Mother and I thought he'd outlive us. Parrots are *supposed* to outlive one. But Tweedy lay down on his back one morning and died. I suppose he had some bird ailment one has never heard of. Well—it was something of a relief for us. After all, what would have happened to him if he *had* outlived us? He was so bad-tempered! Naturally, we miss him. Or her. It is difficult to know about birds."

As she spoke, she was taking eggs, one by one, from a basket and slipping them into a paper sack. She held it out to Mr. Ames. "That will be one Canadian dollar, please," she said, with sardonic emphasis on the word "Canadian." Mr. Ames paid her and he and Catherine started to leave.

"Just a minute," the woman said commandingly. "Would you mind terribly saying a word to my mother? She hardly has any visitors anymore, except when the Reverend Ross stops by. Just as well he doesn't stop too often. He's forever gabbing about food and how people eat it. A tiresome man. A secret glutton, I believe. Fortunately, Mother is quite deaf."

"We'd be delighted," Mr. Ames said, smiling, but the woman had not waited for his answer and did not see his smile. She had taken the lamp and was marching down the hall. They followed her to a room as stuffed with objects as the one they had left. A potbellied stove glowed like a giant ember. In front of it, sitting in a huge collapsed chair that looked like an elephant kneeling, was an ancient woman. Her eyes were closed.

"Mother!" shouted the woman. "The people from the States have come to say good evening to you."

The old lady opened one eye, then the other, like a doll with sticky works.

Mr. Ames pushed some cardboard boxes out of his way and stood in front of her and bowed deeply. In a loud voice, he said, "Delighted to meet you!" Something fell in the dark beyond the glow of the stove and the light of the lamp. Could it have been some other visitor trapped by junk who had not been able to escape the room? Catherine felt a violent surge of laughter. She clenched her jaw. Sweat dripped down her forehead. Her father seemed unable to straighten up. He cast a glance at her, and she tried to back into the hall, but the woman was blocking her way.

She thought she might scream, when the ancient woman suddenly nodded and said in a tiny high voice, "Thank you . . . thank you. Have you seen our Tweedy?"

"Tweedy!" her father shouted as though the parrot's name had some immense significance he had just recollected. I am going to faint, Catherine announced to herself. "I'm hot," she muttered to the big woman. "Must get outside. . . ."

The woman pressed herself against the wall. Catherine shot past her down the hall, through the front room and out of the house. She leaned against the car, gasping with laughter.

She heard the door close; then her father was standing in front of her. "Deserted me in mid-battle," he said reproachfully.

"I was going to burst," she said. "I didn't think you'd ever straighten up again, and you'd be stuck there forever, like Tweedy."

"What a tableau we'd make, Tweedy and I," he said, starting the car.

"What crazy old people."

"Don't condescend."

"I wasn't," she said. "They were crazy."

"You were," he contradicted her. "It doesn't matter if they were crazy."

"But you thought they were funny, too. I could see you did."

"So I did," he acknowledged. "The difference is —I know I could end up the same way in just such a room. You think what we saw there is far from your own fate. Don't be so sure."

She felt put upon. How could she be expected to know what he knew? He was pretty old, after all. She looked over at him. As usual, his grip on the steering wheel was desperate, as though he suspected that the car at any moment might fly off the face of the earth. An impulse of sympathy, so contrary to what she was feeling, made her reach out a hand to touch his sleeve. "I'll take care of you when you're a crone," she said.

"You will, will you!" he exclaimed ferociously. She saw he was smiling.

When they were eating their supper, he told her here was a French expression, *fou rire*, for that uncontrollable laughter that can seize one in the most inappropriate situation. It was just such an attack of "fool's laughter," he said, that had probably driven him into writing. It had happened to him during a high school production of a play, a medieval stew put together by his class and their English teacher. He had been given a walk-on part as the King's guard.

"I wasn't much of a guard," he told her, "since the King was murdered in Act Two. We were dressed in costumes. It was the end of June. I thought I was turning into a pudding. The King was lying in state on his funeral bier, and he was covered from head to toe in ill-fitting sections of tin armor we'd made in shop. His faithful and ancient courtier—and bearded, that's the important detail—leaned over the corpse to say farewell. The courtier was a disreputable pal of mine named Duds, who was having an awful time with his speech, making up most of it since he hadn't been able to memorize more than a line or two. I was beginning to smirk behind my visor when suddenly poor Duds bent too close to the King, who was itching and sweating and wriggling. Anyhow, Dud's long fake beard got caught somewhere in the King's breastplate. He couldn't stand up straight without ripping off the beard. Duds didn't have much feeling for drama, but he knew *that* would be a serious mistake. I've never heard such whispered curses as passed between Duds and the corpse—at the same time, Duds shouted out words of praise for the King's character: Honest! Courteous! True blue! The teacher finally sent four boys out and they picked up the bier with the King on it and Duds bent over him, trapped, and ran offstage, Duds running sideways like a giant bearded crab. The Queen was supposed to make a speech, but she never got to make it. Your daddy was sprawled on the stage on his back just like a beetle, screaming, helpless with *fou rire*. Of course, I was never given another chance at a part. They made me write plays after that. Thus I met my destiny—by backing into it."

"That isn't really why you wrote, is it?" she asked.

"It's as good a reason as any," he said. Then, abruptly changing the subject, he told her he was going to read *The Ancient Mariner* to her when she finished the dishes.

"I had it in school," she said.

"What in God's name does that mean?" he asked irritably. "Had it . . ."

"I mean we had to read it and memorize parts of it."

"That doesn't mean you *had it*. I can't bear that lingo," he said.

After they had eaten their omelets, he went into the parlor. She washed up the dishes, glad to have something ordinary and boring to do. The chore steadied her. She had never been around anyone whose mood could change so quickly.

When she went into the parlor, he was sitting in the armchair, a book opened on his lap. He smiled pleasantly, somewhat remotely.

"Ready for Coleridge?" he asked.

"Ready," she replied.

✿ ✿ ✿ ✿ ✿ ✿ ✿ ✿ Five

HE BEGAN to grow restless. In the night, she heard him moving about the little house. Sometimes he took care not to disturb her sleep; at other times he walked heavily through the rooms and turned on all the downstairs lights. She lay awake, staring at her doorway and the dimly illuminated passage beyond it. She listened to his footsteps, the jarring of furniture when he bumped into it, and she felt disquieted, confused, by his voiceless presence below.

Once, at four a.m., unable to fall back to sleep

when the house had grown silent again, she went downstairs to find him reading intently in the parlor, an opened bottle of club soda on the floor by his foot. He looked at her briefly. "Back to bed with you, Brunhilde," he said. "Leave me to my wars."

Only a long time later, when she was back in school, did it occur to her that his "wars," his trouble, had been about liquor.

They did a good deal of driving: to Lake Rossignol, often to Halifax, or they would follow a country road for miles, pausing in one of the villages they passed through to buy a lunch of cheese and crackers and apples, eating it in a field by the side of the road. Whatever it was that kept him wakeful at night, he appeared to Catherine to be calmer in the day as they drove about the countryside without any special destination, or as they sat among clumps of wildflowers in those stubbly fields talking of this or that. There were even hours when she took his presence for granted and so, in a way, forgot him.

The place she liked best of all was a tiny fishing village perched on a cove that opened out into the Atlantic Ocean. They spent an afternoon there, climbing across great beige-colored rocks, stopping to watch the water sweep into narrow crevices, investigating tidal pools. Beneath their motionless, mucky surfaces, the little pools swarmed with minute life. He told her about the creatures that lived in them.

Looking at her quizzically, he said, "Surprised, aren't you, that I know about such things? I know a lot that doesn't matter—to me, that is. My brain is like an old attic. I wander through it, picking up one thing or another, hoping to be interested."

It was not his knowledge that had surprised her so much as the odd revulsion he showed toward the rock-trapped greenish pools; as he pointed to a plant, or a tiny creature wriggling about it, one hand hovered just above the water and the other gripped the rough rock. He seemed to read her face, to know she was puzzled by something about him. "The teeming earth," he murmured.

The sea glittered like a cloth of gold. Beyond the curve of a narrow jetty, its movement was slow and soft. The sky was cloudless. Fishing shacks on stilts strode the water like long-legged birds. A woman hung men's workclothes on a rope stretched from a hook in the weathered shingle of her house to a pole that looked like a mast. Little islands of brilliant green grass grew in sand. There was a glitter of seashells on paths that led to the painted blue doors of the houses along the single narrow road. Except

for the woman, the only other person they saw was
an old man sitting in a rowboat near a ramshackle
dock. He looked asleep.

"The men are out fishing. The women wait within,"
said Mr. Ames.

"Maybe it's the other way around," Catherine said.

"Ha!" exclaimed her father.

The water, the rocks, the weathered shacks were
like washes of pure color. "I love it here," she said.

"Someday I'll take you to the Shetland Islands,"
he said.

When she was around twelve, during one of their
restaurant meetings, he'd told her about a boarding
school in Lausanne, Switzerland. She would love it
there, he had promised. "Little international girls,"
he said. "Much more grown-up than their American
counterparts." She was jealous at once.

He'd buy her a steamer trunk, the old-fashioned
kind people used to take on long voyages on the great
ships that used to sail to all the ports in the world.
She could pack it with wonderful things and sail
away to France. He'd meet her there. They would
drive through Burgundy and over the Jura Alps. The
school was on a hill that overlooked Lake Geneva.
She'd learn marvelous things in that school.

"What things?" she had asked.

"Languages, for one," he told her. "French, Italian. You'll see how differently people look at the world. You won't be locked up inside your own language."

"Don't people talk and think about the same things?"

"No, they don't," he said. "I want you to learn how big the world is, how various. It's said to be small; people are said to be the same everywhere. It's not. They're not."

The steamer trunk took hold of her imagination. She expected it somehow to turn up in the apartment where she lived with her mother, the same one where her father had once lived, too.

One afternoon after school, she found a luggage shop. In the window sat an enormous trunk, its top open to show a floral-papered interior. Resting against the top was a huge, cream-colored fan painted with Roman arches and flowers. Across the trunk's rim rested a pair of long ivory-colored gloves. Grouped around the steamer trunk were canvas bags and plastic suitcases. She suddenly understood that the trunk was like a suit of armor—or a dinosaur—and was part of a story her father was always telling her, a story of yesterday. After that, when he spoke about places he would take her "someday," she began to believe that she would only reach them by traveling backward in time, into the past, his past.

They sat down on the pier and watched the old man, awake now, as he fished from the side of his boat.

"Perhaps not the Shetlands," her father was saying reflectively. "That's for when you're older, when you're not looking outward so much as you do now, quite naturally—"

"I don't know what you mean," she interrupted him, with sudden irritation.

"Now, now, child! Don't be cross-tempered. You know that everything I say is true. I'll tell you what I mean. The older you get, the less you'll be interested in what is outside you."

"I may be different from you," she said sharply.

She saw how he looked at her then, with real curiosity, and it was that she believed in—not his promises.

"I bet you are," he said with conviction. "God knows, I hope you are. Look! He's caught something."

Slowly, sedately, the old man reeled in his line until the struggling fish, wrenched out of its own element, hung glistening in the air. The old man unhooked it, dropped it in the boat, and cast out his line again.

"What pleases you most in the world?" her father asked.

She loved his questions. Her answers often surprised her as much as they seemed to surprise him. She pondered as they sat there on the warm splintery wood of the dock, their legs dangling over the side above the water shushing gently among the pilings. It was hard to think of anything that could please her more than this moment. She gave it a try, thought of one thing or another, picking over pleasures as though they were candies in a box, until she recalled the performance of a troupe of Spanish dancers the Dalraida girls had been taken to see that winter.

The premier male dancer, dressed in black, had stood on the stage as straight as a column, slim as a birch tree, his hands raised above his head to clap the quickening beat. She thought of a movie she'd seen, set in Greece, and a scene of men dancing with their arms around one another's waists in the vine-hung courtyard of a *taverna*, and she thought of Philippe in his ski boots in front of the mountain village chapel where people went to have their skis blessed. It was midnight; a single lamp glittered in the frosty air. He did a wild clog dance, a burlesque of a folk dance. They had laughed so much; they had fallen into a snowdrift, their arms around each other, shouting with hilarity, with their delight in each other.

"Men, dancing," she said at last.

He was staring intently at her. As she spoke, he turned his face away quickly but not before she had seen some profound sadness in his face. He patted her shoulder. "You're a dear," he said.

They walked slowly back to the car, which he had parked just outside the village. "Where I most want to take you is Italy," he said. "I won't drag you through museums—you can't tell what you're looking at after a while. We'll follow one painter from the place he was born to all the churches where he left a fresco or a painting. That's how you'll really see. How you'll love the countryside! The Chianti hills, the Alps of the Moon, the cities, Siena and Arezzo, Sansepolcro, Urbino, Assisi . . ."

The names rang through the village silence like deep-throated bells. She expected people to come out of their houses and applaud.

"I mean it this time, Cath," he said. "I know I've built up your expectations before—and disappointed them. But I always truly believed it would all happen. Now I mean it to. Emma and you and me. What good times we'll have! But you must finish your schooling first so as not to alarm the guardians of our lives."

She didn't ask him what school, whether he meant high school or college or graduate school, or if he would arrive—at last!—with tickets and hotel reservations when she was working and the mother of six children.

She had realized that for her father, talking itself was an event, a journey. But, at least, she was with him now. That had really come true. The skimpy little house on a scruffy cliff was not Italy, not the Shetlands. But in the cramped rooms where they had talked so much, it seemed to her that a promise had been fulfilled.

She wondered if he knew that.

꽃 꽃

Although nineteen days had passed, the time had seemed to stretch only through one long afternoon. She had begun to learn ordinary things about him: his indifference to clothes but his pleasure in the English shoes he had made for himself once every two years, his comical rages at his inability to stop smoking, his voice in the morning, the boisterous way he cooked and the rather delicate way he ate, what his face looked like when he was tired.

One Saturday morning as she washed up the breakfast dishes, she realized she wanted to go off by herself. The hours had been so precious to her when she'd met him for visits, she hadn't even wanted to take the time to go to the bathroom.

"I think I'll make a sandwich and go down that road where we went shooting," she said.

He looked amused. "Had enough, have you?" he asked.

She started to explain—then didn't know what it was she wanted to explain. She felt apprehensive. Had she hurt his feelings?

"Splendid idea," he said. "Me, too. I'll take some time off. We can afford that now, can't we?"

She made herself a peanut butter sandwich and put it in a bag with an apple and a bottle of water. He had brought her a copy of D. H. Lawrence's novel *The Lost Girl*, and she stuffed the paperback into the pocket of her jeans. As she went out the door, he called after her, "Be sure to come back! Don't join some traveling troupe of actors!"

She began to run and didn't stop until she was out of sight of the house. At the top of her lungs, she sang an Aznavour song she'd memorized. Her voice echoed and was lost in the hills, and she stopped singing, content with the silence. She ambled down the road they'd walked, and far beyond the place where they had turned back, until there wasn't even a track. She strode through a great meadow full of Queen Anne's lace and black-eyed Susans. On a mossy mound beneath a tree, she sat down and ate her lunch.

In a painful moment, she felt a touch of fear, of anxiety—she was losing time she might have spent with him. But the sense of her aloneness filled her with a kind of exultation. She stared up through the leaves at the sky. After a while she opened her book, though she didn't attempt to read. A breeze stirred her hair. She heard from nearby the steady work-manlike buzz of insects. She felt herself sink into mindlessness, felt the edge of sleep, and then it broke over her like a slow wave.

When she woke up, the paper lunch bag was caught on a thistle a few yards away. The sun had moved a long distance westward. She must have slept a day and a night! How tired she had been! She grabbed up the bag, the book, and started back to the house, eager to see what he'd been up to all this time. It must have been three or four hours that she'd been away. At breakfast, he'd said something about going to a movie that evening. Maybe they could find one in Lunenberg, the nearest large town, one they hadn't yet visited.

The car was parked in a different place. He had probably gone into the village to get groceries. What would he cook that night? She felt famished.

At the back door she paused. The house was so silent. He had been tired, too. Perhaps he had taken a nap and was still sleeping. Then she heard his voice. The words were indistinct, but the tone, as soft and sweet as caramel, carried to where she stood. She opened the door and went into the parlor. "Oh!" she said.

A woman was leaning forward in the old armchair. Mr. Ames was standing behind it, his hands resting on its curved back. The woman started to get up. Mr. Ames touched her shoulder and she sank back into the chair. "Here's my big girl!" he greeted Catherine loudly, and walked over to her, putting his arm around her shoulder and drawing her further into the room. The woman smiled uneasily, looking from Mr. Ames to Catherine with a dazed, helpless expression on her face. She looked away from them and began to smooth the skirt of her light cotton dress.

"Catherine, this is Mrs. Conklin . . . you remember her husband . . . you met him recently."

"I must be going," Mrs. Conklin said in a timid voice, as she stood, holding tightly to the arm of the chair.

"Mrs. Conklin dropped by to talk something over with me—" he began, but realized his mistake when Mrs. Conklin gave him a stricken look. "What *is* the matter with me? I mean to say—I picked her up in Mackenzie. She's been concerned about her husband's drinking—"

Catherine cleared her throat, croaked out, "Yes . . ." and turned to leave the room.

But Mr. Ames grabbed her arm. "Come along with us. I'll drive her home. I have to pick up the lamb anyhow."

Catherine said, "Thanks"—though she didn't know for what—for his reminding her of supper? She ran upstairs.

Her father called out to her with a kind of maniacal cheerfulness, "Be right back, my girl!"

From her room, she listened to the horrible grinding of gears. Starting the car always agitated him. It sounded now as though he were tearing it apart with a chain saw. There was one last screech before the gears engaged, then a rumble, then silence. She ran downstairs into the kitchen and gulped down a glass of water. In her mind's eye, she saw Mrs. Conklin's pale, almost pretty face, her close-set dark eyes turned beseechingly up to Mr. Ames. What had he been up to?

She knew what he'd been up to. "He's married," she whispered aloud. "He's old."

She had heard that caramel tone in his voice even when he spoke to Mrs. Landy. He wanted everyone to be in love with him, Reverend Ross, the village bums. He'd show up next with the farmer's wife, romancing her, too. She twisted away from the sink and sat down at the table. Her head felt full of gravel. He was disgusting! The world traveler, stomping through Mackenzie with his big belly, his actor's voice, showing the hicks what a star he was!

She went outside to the swing and stood next to it, her hand on the sun-warmed wood slats, taking deep breaths the way she did before the dentist gave her a needle. The swallows had begun their late-afternoon flight over the meadow. She watched them for a long time, until they seemed to be flying inside her head, and she felt quiet and somewhat comforted. She went back to the kitchen and made herself a large sandwich. She didn't need him to feed her.

"Catherine?"

He was standing in the doorway, looking at her.

"Whatever you think—you're wrong," he said.

"Mrs. Conklin just dropped in," she said coldly. "By parachute, I guess."

"You might take note of how ineptly I lie," he said. "That ought to reassure you."

"Is that what telling lies is for?"

"You don't know how empty people's lives can be," he said.

"Is Emma's life empty?" she asked, not looking at him.

"Emma doesn't expect me to make her life full,"

he replied, but his voice had faltered a little. "I wasn't intending to run off with that young woman," he went on. "I was spending an hour or so with her. It's true that I ran into her in the grocery store in Mackenzie. I'm from far away, an outsider, someone she can talk to." He paused. When he continued, his voice was louder, more confident. "She did want to talk to me about his drinking. And I know a bit about that."

That was like asking the wolf for advice about how to protect the sheep, Catherine thought to herself. What she said was, "You didn't look like you'd been talking."

He laughed, throwing back his head. "My God! I've sired a Puritan. Do you know about Puritans? It was remarked about them that they objected to bearbaiting as a sport—not because it gave pain to the bears but because it gave pleasure to the spectators. Is that what you're like?"

"None of it's my business," she said angrily.

"Oh, indeed! You'll think your own thoughts, will you? Listen. I wouldn't take up with anyone whose eyes are so close-set. It's a sign of a treacherous nature, Catherine. I'm not a tempter . . . ravening through the countryside. Do you think all I want to do is win people? Beguile them?"

"Yes!" she cried. "Yes, I do!"

He sat down suddenly at the kitchen table, banged his knee against a table leg, and exclaimed, "Ouch!" making a pained face at her. She didn't believe that *ouch*, either.

"You were coming on to her. I saw—"

"Listen to me," he interrupted. "Don't use that junk language to me! 'Coming on to her . . .' I'd rather have you grunt like an ape than use such locutions."

"I don't know what that means," she said, feeling a certain satisfaction that she'd made him angry.

"Look it up," he said gruffly.

"When I have the time," she replied.

He laughed suddenly. It disconcerted her. "All right," she said grudgingly. "Then you were flirting."

"That's better," he said. "In this case, it's untrue. But do you think your old father is past such things? You think flirting is only legal when it's done by the young and beautiful? You'd better get something straight. People flirt on their way to the guillotine."

"I'm going for a walk."

"You've been for a walk," he said sternly. "Anyhow, you had better not leave me alone. I might drive off and grab Mrs. Landy and cozy up to her with ginger beer and forget-me-nots. You'd do much better to peel those potatoes in that bag over there. I slave for you night and day over a hot stove and you don't lift a finger. Here! Take the knife in hand! Peel! I dare say there are scandalous goings-on in that school of yours that would turn your father's hair white with shock!"

He was running all over her, drowning her in language. Still, she felt better. How did he do it? How did he make things that seemed to signify so insignificant? She even had to turn away so he wouldn't see her grin because she was thinking about Mrs. Landy and ginger beer and forget-me-nots. She peeled the potatoes and sliced them thinly as he directed her to do, and was gratified when he praised her work.

He didn't offer to read to her that evening. He had some work of his own to do, he said. Once, unbidden, the face of Mrs. Conklin interposed itself between her eyes and the pages of the Lawrence novel she was reading. She glanced over at him. He had drawn up a small table to his armchair, and he was bent over some pages of typing, a pencil in one hand, his expression concentrated. He seemed to sense her scrutiny. He looked up and smiled at her.

"Can't anyone be happy?" she asked.

"Oh, yes," he answered at once. "Yes . . . yes." He reached out his hand as he often did when he read poetry. "We've been happy here. And you *will* be happy. I know that. Someone said that hope itself is a kind of happiness." He hesitated a moment, then went on. "When I lash out at life, it's because I'm so disappointed in myself."

She was grateful for his words, even more grateful for the return of her affection for him. "It's when you don't think about happiness," he said gently, "that it suddenly comes." He smiled again and turned his attention back to his work.

"I am happy *now*," she told herself as she went up the stairs to bed.

It was a gray morning. The rain began to fall just as Mr. Ames and Catherine finished their breakfast. "I have to call Mom today," she said.

"They're back, then?" he asked.

"They're supposed to be," she replied.

As she washed up the dishes, she looked through the window at the heavy rain, remembering how they had walked down the dirt road on a morning that seemed so long ago. Only a few days left! Yet she didn't feel sad when she imagined herself back in New York, free to go out and wander around. She would go to the Museum of Natural History, to the great hall of the mastodons where she had spent so many hours as a child staring at the immense, motionless creatures in their amber-lit landscapes. She would be glad to be back in school, listening to Madame Soule talk passionately about the state of the world, about what could be done for whales and seals, for peace, things that were not about personal life but about life itself. When she thought now of the whole living, buzzing hive of girls, each one so different from the other, she felt a rush of eagerness to see them, which even included dangerous Harriet. And there was Philippe. She could visualize him walking toward her on Sherbrooke Street, to the bookstore where they often met, so quick, so light on his feet. She was to telephone him tomorrow. He would be waiting for her call in the office of the lumber company in Trois Rivières, which had hired him for the summer. He had given her a piece of paper with a cartoon of himself in a woodsman's outfit, a beard down to his knees, and the telephone number and date and time when she was to call. She always carried it with her, and she took it from her pocket now and looked at it. The paper was smudged from much handling. Her father walked up to stand next to her.

"Secret messages?" he asked. She put the paper away hurriedly.

"It's nothing," she said. Through the window, she saw a man in uniform walking over the rise to the house. He stepped across the railroad track just as Mrs. Landy appeared a few yards behind him. He paused and waited for her. They spoke together as though they knew each other.

"A soldier?" Catherine inquired of her father.

"That's the Royal Canadian Mounted Policeman," he answered. "Around here, they'd call him a RCMP."

"Where's his horse?"

"Obsolete," said Mr. Ames.

"They're both getting soaked."

"They don't mind weather like us sissies," he said.

"I like rain," she said defensively.

A moment or so later, Mrs. Landy entered the kitchen, sighing out her usual, "Good day," and adding, "RCMP to see you, Mr. Ames." She took off her wet head scarf and wrung it out over the sink.

Mr. Ames, Catherine following him, went to the door.

The mountie was very young. His face was red as though he blushed perpetually, his eyes deep blue, the pale eyebrows above them the color of wheat. He announced himself to be Macbeth and gave a half salute.

Mr. Ames clapped him on the back and exclaimed, "Wonderful!"

Macbeth looked mildly surprised.

"Have some coffee with us, laddie," offered Mr. Ames.

"I wouldn't mind—with the rain and all," Macbeth said shyly.

He stood woodenly in the parlor, staring at the floor, while Catherine tried to think of something interesting to say. Whatever he was looking at seemed to absorb him entirely. Mr. Ames returned with a tole tray and three cups of coffee.

"What can we do for you, Officer Macbeth?" he asked genially. "I hope that's the proper way to speak to you. Where did you get that marvelous name?"

"It's an old family name," replied Macbeth stolidly. "There's lots of Macbeths in these parts, cousins of mine and all. Well, thank you for the coffee." He drank down the whole contents of the cup in one gulp. "What I've come to ask you is—have you noticed anybody walking around here with a rifle? There's been a complaint back there in the hills along Ross Road. Barn windows have been shot out."

"Ross Road?" inquired Mr. Ames blandly. "Would the Reverend Ross own that road?"

"Different family," said Macbeth.

"We haven't seen a soul," Mr. Ames said definitely. "My daughter and I are visitors here. In fact, we're returning to the States in a few days. Do sit down, Macbeth. Can I get you some more coffee? Would you like a bit of Lamb's rum in it?"

Catherine shot a stricken glance at him. He hadn't thrown out all the liquor.

"Thanks, no," Macbeth said. "I took the pledge. I used to drink something terrible."

"An honest answer," Mr. Ames observed ponderously.

At least, he hadn't been drinking the rum, Catherine told herself. She would have known if he had, wouldn't she? He was asking Macbeth if it was true that the woods were full of bootleggers and the barns full of illegal stills. Macbeth smiled at him and looked even younger. Catherine went off to the kitchen. The conversation was making her uneasy.

Mrs. Landy was wiping down the counter. "How's Jackie?" Catherine asked. She could hear the rumble of her father's voice, Macbeth's clear, mild tones as he replied. Her father would be charming the mountie the way he did everyone—everyone except the Reverend Ross.

"Little Jackie's just fine," Mrs. Landy said.

"We drove to Lake Rossignol," Catherine offered.

"That's nice," Mrs. Landy said, wiping the front of the stove. "It's nice to go to a lake."

Mrs. Landy could provide a new definition of what a conversation was, Catherine thought.

Her father called out an exuberant good-bye to Macbeth. She went back into the parlor. As she passed the kitchen table, she saw Mrs. Landy's worn black pocketbook lying on it, open. To her surprise, she glimpsed a large, cellphane-wrapped cigar lying on a neatly folded pink tissue.

"Mrs. Landy smokes cigars," she whispered to her father.

"Good night! How hearty of her! I'm relieved she has a vice," he whispered back.

He looked very pleased with himself, she noticed. How quickly and easily he had lied. But what if he had been truthful? She could just see the scene in a Canadian courtroom—American visitors convicted of mindless hooliganism. The judge would be someone like Harriet Blacking, who always spoke about "those boors to the south of us," and had once called the United States "the United Snakes."

"You lie so fast," she said, trying to speak impersonally, like a judge, but not succeeding. "You were too charming."

"My trouble has always been that I'm too charming," he said. "Never mind that. I'm not trying to set you an example. Don't tell lies because I do. You have the choice, you know. Isn't Macbeth a nice young fellow? Not the usual antagonistic upholder of the law. He looked at you with considerable interest. He doesn't give a fig for barn windows. You're the reason he bothered to stay so long."

"He didn't notice me," she said.

"Don't simper," he said. "Why shouldn't he notice you? The thing is—he's coming back to drive us around this evening when he goes off duty."

"Drive us around where?"

"A few places he thought would be interesting," he replied evasively.

She didn't press him; she was afraid of what he might tell her. If he intended to go to bootleggers, she understood that she couldn't prevent him from doing so. The tenderness she knew he felt toward her did not alter a hardness of purpose in him where his own wish was concerned. She had not known that drinking could carry you out of reach of your own feelings for people. She hadn't known anything about drinking. But she felt she must say something that would let him know what was on her mind.

"You didn't tell me you kept the Lamb's rum."

"I'm not obliged to make reports to you," he said flatly. "In any event, rum is not my drink. It's for visitors."

She didn't look at him as she asked for the car

keys so she could drive to Mackenzie to telephone her mother. She didn't want to see his face.

"Say hello to her for me," he said neutrally.

She wouldn't.

The public telephone in the village was on the wall of a narrow lunchroom that smelled of ketchup and stale coffee. She felt sad and disheartened and disgruntled as she asked the operator to put through a collect call. The one waitress behind the counter handed a hamburger as thin as a wafer to a man in workclothes.

When she heard her mother's eager voice accepting the charges, her spirits rose. "Oh! I'm so glad you're home!" she exclaimed.

"What's the matter? Is anything the matter?" her mother asked, her voice filled with alarm.

"No, no. I'm just glad to hear you," Catherine said. "I was afraid you might have already started back to work, and that switchboard operator in your office wouldn't have accepted the charges—" She broke off. Why was she having to explain everything? "I'm fine," she said, "really great. How was your trip?"

"Marvelous. I've got so much to tell you and show you. We took hundreds of pictures. How was Toronto?"

"Toronto?" asked Catherine, her mind blank. Then

she remembered. "Oh, Toronto. Pretty nice. Not as nice as here."

"I'm so happy you'll be home soon."

"Yes," agreed Catherine.

"Yes? Yes, what? Catherine, you sound—"

"I'm happy, too," Catherine broke in hastily.

"Is he behaving himself?" her mother asked, her voice grim.

Would her mother ever stop prosecuting the case against her father? Did she want a chorus of ten thousand voices crying out that she had been the only injured party? Right now, her father was licking his chops, everything drained out of his head except for the thought of moonshine liquor. Her wayward parents!

But she realized, if only fleetingly, that it had been hard for her mother to let her spend this time with Mr. Ames. If she knew he had kept Catherine waiting for three weeks!

"Mom, he's being really fine. He cooks terrific meals. We've been all over the place. I'm really okay. Mom?"

Driving back to the house, thinking of how she had calmed her mother's self-serving fears, she felt exiled to a chilly place, far from those parents of hers.

❧ ❧ ❧ ❧ ❧ ❧ ❧ ❧ Six

CATHERINE, washing supper dishes, saw a rabbit through the kitchen window. Suddenly it dropped down on all fours and fled. Macbeth walked out of the lingering sunlight and into the shadow of the peaked roof that nearly reached the railroad tracks. Even as she pronounced his name, she heard the door bang shut.

He came down the hall and into the kitchen, her father leading him. He looked like a child dressed up for an occasion, in a tight tweed jacket and a yellow necktie.

"Evening," he said to her shyly. She nodded.

"Come into the parlor while my staff finishes up in here," her father said jovially. She felt a flash of resentment. His joking was a part of their private conversation. In front of a stranger, the joke was stripped of affection. She heard only his words, and they seemed derisive and harsh.

She didn't want to go anywhere with Macbeth. She had asked Mr. Ames if she could stay home. "I want you with us," he had said. It wasn't his words that prevented her from arguing it out with him. She had sensed uneasiness in his voice, in the way he looked at her, as though he were afraid.

She had wanted to ask him about his writing that evening, although she hadn't figured out how to bring it up. She knew it was a thorny subject.

Her mother had kept a copy of his first novel in a row of cookbooks on a kitchen shelf. Several years ago, Catherine had taken it off to her room. Her mother had found her reading it at her desk, her school books pushed aside.

"You'd do better to do your homework," she commented.

Catherine didn't answer. She rarely responded to

her mother's remarks about her father. She had held onto the book, not looking up. Her mother said, sharply, that he had written a second novel but it wasn't any good. The first one was all right—but then his true character had caught up with him. Despite herself, Catherine couldn't help asking what that was? Her mother looked confused, as though she hadn't expected to have to explain what she meant. She picked up a jacket Catherine had dropped on the floor and began to fold it like a towel.

"He thinks being hopeless about life is romantic, deep," her mother said. "That's what's wrong with his books."

"Is he hopeless?" Catherine asked.

"It's a pose."

"Then you mean—he's not really hopeless?" Catherine asked relentlessly.

Her mother dropped the jacket on a chair. "Oh —I don't know," she said agitatedly. "He baffled me so. . . ."

It was, Catherine had thought at the time, nearly the only kind thing her mother had ever said about her father.

The novel related the adventure of a young man who got a job as a cabin boy on a tramp steamer going to South America. She read it to hear her father's voice. It was the first time since she had learned to read that she realized a real, living person had written a book.

She had spent months poking around in second-hand book stores. At last, in the basement of one of them, a place that smelled of dust and stale paper and decay, she found his second novel. It was just over one hundred pages long. It ended so abruptly, so mysteriously, it was as though the writer had dropped his manuscript and left town forever. The story began with a terrible accident. A man was hit by a train. He had walked a mile before he collapsed and died. The life in him had not recognized its time was up. Some earlier reader than Catherine had underlined a sentence on the last page: *We want to keep on living even as we are ground to dust*.

She found his travel books everywhere. In them were listed places to eat and stay, bits of history about castles and town halls and notable personalities, written in a tone of hard-boiled commercial cheerfulness, as though the main object of visiting other countries was to find good room service and good plumbing. "For *arrivistes*," he had told her, "people who only want to know about the most expensive restaurants and hotels."

She heard him now in the parlor. He was speaking

in a loud, hearty voice; it had in it an insistence that everything was about to be wonderful.

"Get a jacket or something, Cath," he called to her as she went down the hall to the stairs. "Macbeth says there's a touch of autumn in the air." Telling her to get something to keep herself warm was one of the few ways in which he behaved like a parent, she noted. Then she thought—autumn! They had only a few days left!

As Catherine joined them in the parlor, Macbeth was saying, "Please, Mr. Ames, call me Alistair."

"Actually, I think of it as a privilege to call you Macbeth."

"From the play by William Shakespeare," Catherine said, with a touch of grimness.

" 'False face must hide what the false heart doth know,' " recited Macbeth in a schoolboy's singsong voice.

"By God!" exclaimed Mr. Ames. "You're a barrel of surprises, Macbeth!"

"I read it in school. We had to memorize bits," said Macbeth modestly.

It was *she* who had been patronizing, she realized. Until that moment, she had thought her father's obscure allusions had been a kind of showing off to himself, showing himself how much he knew that other people didn't. But thinking back to the time they'd spent with Reverend Ross, with Mr. Conklin and Farmer Glimm, and, of course, with Mrs. Landy, she guessed that they hadn't felt patronized at all. He didn't think he was superior because of what he knew. She did. Ashamed, she went to him. He put his arm around her. "My dear," he said, his voice surprised.

Macbeth drove a small English car. Catherine curled up in the back seat. There wasn't enough room for her legs, so she had to squeeze herself up like an accordion. Mr. Ames didn't stop talking for one moment. There was an undercurrent of excitement in his voice that must, Catherine imagined, make the little car glow like a coal as they drove through the countryside upon which night had now fallen.

Macbeth turned onto a dirt road. The car shuddered and bounced and clattered. A few hundred yards ahead of them, Catherine could see a cluster of dim lights. Macbeth parked. They sat in silence for a moment or two. "Interesting," Mr. Ames said in a subdued voice. What on earth was he really thinking? she wondered.

"Well, you walk right over there to the barn," Macbeth said. "Tell them Alistair sent you."

"Not Macbeth?" asked Mr. Ames, already half out of the car.

"Oh, no," Macbeth replied. "Don't say my last name. They know who it is, but I only use Macbeth when it's an official visit. When I have to close them down, do you see?"

"Strange distinction," Mr. Ames commented, staring at Catherine. "Take note. It's an example of the social contract."

"Not really," she muttered. He seemed not to have heard her. She watched him walk away, saw his shadow loom against the barn door.

"What's in there?" she asked.

"It's a fellow does a little bootlegging. A potato farmer who earns a bit of money that way."

"A still, you mean?"

"That's right. In the line of work I know about these places." He turned toward her. She smelled his mint-flavored breath.

"But it's illegal. Don't you arrest bootleggers?" she asked. She felt helpless, crouched there behind him.

"Yes, I do arrest them. Not on my time off, though. After a while, they start up all over again. It's the laws that are wrong. The farmers know they can be arrested, and they know some judge could make it hard for them. They're poor people mostly. They need the extra money."

"What about when they don't need extra money?"

"I don't know about that," he replied indifferently. "Your father was saying he might write a book about us here, about Nova Scotia, and that's why he wanted to know about the bootlegging. Get the flavor of the place—so to speak."

She squeezed herself tighter into the seat. What a fool Macbeth was! Chewing a mint to make himself sweet, putting on his buttercup tie—didn't he know what was up? Would he believe her if she shouted at him that her father was on a tear, that he wanted to drink up every still for miles around?

"I've got to get out of this back seat. I feel like a pretzel," she said.

He was quick to help her out, gripping her wrist with his warm, hard hand. She was being unfair to him. Her father was making everything turn bad.

They stood silently in the moist air. He lit a cigarette. Only the blurred light from the barn showed there was anyone else abroad in the night. There wasn't any noise coming from there at all.

"You go to school here in Canada?" Macbeth whispered.

"Yes," she answered loudly. She wanted the bootlegger to know there was someone out here. The barn door opened; a ray of light fell on the ground. She saw her father coming back. She got into the car at once.

"Fascinating!" Mr. Ames said expansively. "What an extraordinary process! It's been going on forever, of course. I wonder if you know, Macbeth, that in Sweden there's a limit on profits you can make from liquor. Ethically sound but absolutely senseless."

Macbeth nodded but said nothing as they drove to the tarmac road.

"I hope you got a sample," Catherine said.

"Indeed, I did," replied Mr. Ames quickly. "And delicious it was. I had to test the product . . . quite a bit like gasoline, I imagine."

"Cranshaw's new at it," Macbeth said apologetically.

"All the same to me, lad," said Mr. Ames with an easy laugh.

They drove down other rough roads. Once Catherine was flung up and hit her head on the roof.

"I beg your pardon," said Macbeth.

"Ow!" cried her father in a falsetto voice.

How she hated them both!

As they waited for Mr. Ames outside a large shed, rain began to fall. Macbeth tried once more to engage her in conversation. "Where is your school?" he asked.

"Montreal," she replied, and not a word more.

The enmity she felt toward him, unjust as she knew it to be, had the effect of making her feel as old as he was. She heard him sigh. She didn't feel a touch of sympathy for him. He was a country cop who now and then arrested a farmer. He was someone her father was making a fool of.

Yet she felt a contrary emotion; she wanted to apologize to him, to tell him everything. They were nearly the same age. Her father was an old pirate. They might just drive off and leave him in that shed with the still and the bootlegger. Let him talk to the bootlegger about social contracts!

Mr. Ames returned. He got into the car, talking. His arms waved. For Macbeth's benefit, she guessed, he told the story of the man who lived in a lighthouse, the one whose appendix had burst. But he changed the ending. The man walked eight miles only to die on the steps of a village post office. She was as shocked as though she'd known that man, and her father had betrayed him, killed him.

Mr. Ames turned to look at her. "Lots of endings to a story," he said challengingly.

They stopped at one more place, a garage behind a pool hall just outside of Halifax. It was raining hard now, and she and Macbeth went into the pool hall to wait. Her father had seemed more or less sober until that moment. As he walked past the pool table, and a coffee bar where a lone man sat reading a torn newspaper, he began to stagger suddenly, as if something invisible to the eye were striking him, his shoulders, his back, his arms. "Daddy," she muttered. It almost seemed as if he had heard her. He turned, straightening up, smiled vaguely, and waved in her direction.

The dark street ran with rain. Across it, in a farmhouse set back from the road, a light flickered like a candle in a draft. She leaned against the pool table, her hand on the green baize, picking at its surface.

She had to try to keep still, to keep calm. There would be tomorrow; this night would end.

Macbeth was lighting another cigarette.

"I've never been to New York," he said. "Just went to Augusta, Maine, once." He looked at her hopefully. Still trying.

"In New York there's a bar on every corner and three in the middle of every block," she said, with so much anger she was sure he ducked, as though she'd hurled some object at him.

He went to the door and threw his cigarette into the street. When he turned back, she saw how troubled his broad face was. He shook his head. "I didn't know he'd drink so much," he said, in a low voice. "I thought he was mostly going to see how the stills worked."

She heard her father shout incoherently. Catherine ran to the back of the pool hall and stepped across a narrow cement walk to the threshold of the garage.

Mr. Ames was on his hands and knees barking like a dog. An elderly woman who was leaning against a pile of tires was laughing, her mouth wide open, a gold tooth gleaming under the dim light of a single bulb that hung down from the raw wood ceiling. Next to her stood a short, skinny man with work pants rolled up around his thin shanks, his feet in heavy muddy boots. His lips clenched, he seemed to taste something bitter. Another woman, even older than the first, was sitting in a straight-backed chair, bent forward with laughter. Slowly, one by one, their faces turned toward her. In a dark corner was the shadowed still, most of it covered by tarpaulin. She saw part of a boiler, a spiral pipe, and on the floor several fruit juice bottles filled with copper-colored liquid.

"I want to go home," she said urgently. "Daddy. Please." Her voice broke. The skinny man smiled faintly as though she might be part of the joke of this grotesque American on his knees in front of them. But the woman in the chair stood up in an efficient way, smoothing her housedress, looking at a large man's watch on her wrist.

"Now, Mr. Ames, daughter has come for you,"

she said. "Time to be off with young Alistair out there."

The skinny man darted forward and grabbed her father by his shoulders and lifted him up and held him there, his head lolling. "The women . . ." he mumbled. "They call the tune, right, lads?"

Macbeth came to help lug the shapeless bundle of Mr. Ames back through the poolroom and into the car. The pool hall light went off. Macbeth was speaking; she didn't listen. All the way home, Catherine held onto her father's shoulders so he wouldn't slip forward against the windshield. He muttered from time to time, his words indistinguishable.

It was after midnight when Macbeth parked in the yard. They pulled Mr. Ames from the car and pushed him up the staircase and into his room. Macbeth aimed him at his bed and let him drop. His eyes were shut tight but he emitted a series of shrill yelps. At once, he began to snore heavily.

Macbeth continued to stand in the room, his hands in his jacket pockets. "I'm really sorry, Miss," he said.

"Could you go?" she asked urgently.

"I feel terrible. . . ."

"Mr. Macbeth, you gave him the chance. You didn't force him to drink. Please just go away."

"I'd like to see you again," he said, with a kind

of desperation that startled her. "I could show you some beautiful beaches, places a lot of people don't even know about. I mean—nice places."

"Mr. Macbeth, I don't want to ever see you again."

He left then. She went to the window. He tripped on his way to the car. She saw his face when he turned on the ignition. God only knew what he thought about it all.

Mr. Ames had stopped snoring. His breathing grew noisy, labored. She walked to his bed and took off his beautiful cordovan shoes, dropping them on the floor. She removed his jacket, lifting him and turning him on his side. He flailed out violently once. She stood back and watched him settle down, one clenched fist against his cheek. A thick, sour smell rose from him; he reeked like a swamp. Disgusted and frightened, she moved away from him, back to the window.

The silence pressed in, a silence broken only by his stertorous breathing. The farmers all would be sleeping now; they'd earned their few dollars for the night's work. Mr. Ames groaned deeply. Catherine shivered.

Her mother could not have known this about him—this obliteration. That's what it meant—*to pass out*, the heat of life gone. He had passed out from among the living.

"How lonely are the dead," she said silently to herself. Where had that scrap of poetry come from? It didn't matter. What she felt suddenly, intensely, was pity. She tiptoed back to the bed and drew up a thin blanket to cover him. She didn't know why she bothered to tiptoe. The end of the world couldn't have waked him up. She had never seen anyone so drunk, except for a man lying on a sidewalk in New York City. She and her mother and Carter had just come out of a movie theater. The man had risen from a pile of newspapers and staggered after them. Carter clutched them both and hurried them into a taxi.

Mr. Ames coughed, and the cough turned into a bubbling, choking spasm. He began to tremble violently.

Without pausing to think about what she was going to do, Catherine ran down the stairs, found the car keys on the hall table where Mr. Ames usually left them, and went out and started up the car. She drove down the center of the road, faster than she had ever driven, until she came to Mackenzie. In two minutes, she was knocking at Reverend Ross's door.

"My father is sick, drunk," she said when the Reverend opened the door. She was gasping with fear now, a sense that it was too late—everything was too late. Yet she noticed he was wearing a burnoose. What her father had said flashed into her mind—everyone has a hidden life. What if he died on that bed in the little house? Drowning in all he had consumed that night?

"Come in," the Reverend said. He took her arm and led her to a chair in the hall. "Sit there. I'll get dressed and go back with you. If he needs a doctor, we'll take him in to Halifax. Our local fellow has gone out to Moncton to a conference."

She heard his voice upstairs, a woman's voice answering. Her hands were fists in her lap; she was pushing against time, trying to corner it. Ross returned, dressed. As she drove him back to the house, she told him about the bootleggers, how her father had been drinking steadily for four hours.

"I know all about it," the Reverend said. "I know what happens."

"He might be dead," she suddenly cried out, her hands gripping the steering wheel.

"No. He won't be dead. He's a strong fellow," Ross said. "I noticed that about him when we went fishing. His vigor."

She parked and ran into the house, not looking behind her to see whether the Reverend was following. But she heard him, pounding up the stairs just behind her.

Mr. Ames was lying on his back. He had thrown

off the blanket. There was a long tear in his shirt, as though he had tried to rip it off. His breathing was heavy, uneven. But he wasn't choking now. Even though she wasn't alone, she didn't know if she could bear to hear that choking again.

The Reverend stood by the bed, staring down at Mr. Ames. Carefully, as though it were breakable, he lifted her father's hand and held it. A long time seemed to pass. Catherine felt Ross was holding her father to life as one held a swimmer in trouble above the water.

"He'll sleep it off," said the old man. "He's no worse off than many a man I've seen collapsed at midnight, able to get up in a few hours to milk the cows. Yes, they keep doing it until they die from it. They think it's their own will that keeps them drinking." He lowered her father's hand to the bed.

Mr. Ames sat up, his eyes wide open. He didn't appear to see them standing there, watching him. He bent over and gripped his belly, flung himself out of bed, and staggered from the room across the passageway to the bathroom. Ross and Catherine went after him. He was leaning over the toilet bowl, vomiting. The Reverend put one arm around Mr. Ames's waist, the other he pressed across his forehead. Catherine felt the answering, upward movement of her own guts as her father heaved and spat into the bowl. She went to the tub, wet the edge of a cloth, and wiped his face, wiped away the tears of his struggle, her hands entangled with the Reverend's as they tended him.

When they got him back to his bed, Ross said, "I'll get his clothes off, make him more comfortable. He'll be better now with the poison out of him. He'll sleep. Does he have nightclothes somewhere?"

Catherine took a pair of old flannel pajamas from a nail behind the door and handed them to Ross. Mr. Ames mumbled. He grinned dreadfully, his eyes shut. Ross gestured toward her with a certain impatience. "Go, wait," he said.

She went downstairs and sat in the parlor. After several minutes, Ross came down. "He's well away. He'll be all right," he said, looking at her closely. She could tell he was thinking hard about her.

"I thank you so much," she said, barely recognizing her own voice, it was so thin, so calm. "I don't know what I would have done. . . ."

"You would have managed," the Reverend said gravely. "Only, of course, it's better to have—it's a comfort to have someone else about. You can feel more alone in a room with someone who is drunk than if you're by yourself. The women around here often call me. They know what to do with the men when they get in that condition. But I'm a comfort to them." He wasn't boasting. He was simply telling her what was so.

Would her father have laughed at him as he had after their picnic together? She wouldn't ever laugh at him again. Everything he said was so plain and true. Could her father ever comfort someone by just being around?

"It's a shame," Ross was saying, "that you have to see such things at your age. But not altogether a shame. If you can understand it a little. Forgive it. We're all helpless in one way or another. Drinking is a terrible misfortune. If you remember that— Well, I don't know what more to say."

She had been ashamed. Now the shame was gone.

"When I was a young man, I had his trouble," Ross said, staring at her. He seemed about to say something else but he didn't. The night had worn her so, she felt like litmus paper, as though she could take the imprint of words left unsaid. She knew he had been about to speak of religion, of his belief. But he was a man of some tact. She would not have known that if he hadn't come with her tonight.

"We're leaving very soon," she said. "I'll be going home to New York, to my mother. And then back to school."

He walked over to where she sat and pressed her shoulder for a moment. "You'll be all right, too," he said, and went out the door. He was silent during the drive to his house. She was glad for that. There wasn't anything more to say.

Just before he got out of the car, he said, "Perhaps you'll come back and see us one of these days."

She didn't think she would come back, but if she did, she thought she would want to see him again.

She drove home slowly.

Her father was sleeping quietly. His breathing was normal. She cleaned the bathroom, opening a small window over the bathtub to air it out. She washed the toilet bowl and the basin, even the bathtub, then mopped up the floor with a sponge. It was nearly five a.m. when she finally got to bed. She fell asleep at once.

❧ ❧ ❧ ❧ ❧ ❧ Seven

WHEN SHE AWOKE the sun was blazing at her window. It was Saturday. Mrs. Landy would not come today. It was hard to get up but harder to lie in bed, thinking of the day ahead. At last she rose and went to the door of her father's room. He was asleep. The brilliant morning light fell across his face. He looked like a yellowing photograph of himself. There was a stubble of beard on his cheeks. She wouldn't shave him again.

She made herself a cup of tea. Gradually she grew

aware that she was behaving fussily, folding her hands between sips of tea, keeping her feet neatly in place, gazing at a wrinkled apple on the counter, then at a dish towel hanging from a nail, as though she were reflecting deeply.

The truth was, she was scared.

Her father was an elderly man, out of control. How did Emma stay with him? Did she, with all her money, run away in airplanes and limousines unless he promised to stay sober? How would Catherine and he manage to get through the two days left of their time together?

"It's painful to know you're alive," he had said to her, "because then you know you're mortal." That was why people wanted distraction—not to have to feel that life in themselves that would run out some-day. But you had to know it, he had said; it was the only victory a person could have. Had he known he was alive last night when he was crawling around on his hands and knees, barking? She shuddered at the memory of that scene.

He would try to win her. He often spoke of win-ning this person or that the way you won a trophy. People would be disappointed in him—then he would have to "win" them back. She felt a stitch of pity for him, the kind of stitch she got when she had run too fast, forgetting she had a body. And the stitch would remind her of her rib cage, her heart, its vulnerability. Her pity for him was her vulnerability to him. Maybe Harriet was better off sneering and pointing her stubby, fat finger at the world. There was no romance of life for Harriet, no pity in her.

She realized that her father would not have been surprised by the side of Reverend Ross she had seen last night. Although she had been. But her father knew about people, knew they were full of contradictions. What she couldn't bear was how he used his knowledge.

She went outside; it was better to be away from his sleeping presence. The grass was still damp from the rain. She moved around restlessly, from porch to swing to railroad tracks, feeling confined by the small yard. After a while, she returned to the house. She heard a piece of cutlery drop in the kitchen. She heard a thin tuneless whistle. He was trying to carry it off even though he didn't know she was in the hall, listening. She went out, back to the wooden swing. It was very hot, steamy.

She grew aware that she was being watched. She turned toward the house. Her father was standing a few yards away, holding a cup of coffee.

He lifted up the cup as though to toast her and ambled toward the swing. He looked terrible, as though barely able to stay on his feet.

"Good morning, Catherine," he said warily.

She said nothing.

The swing quivered as he stepped into it and sat down with a thump.

"What an adventure! Like Prohibition days, I imagine. Of course, you and I wouldn't know about that."

She looked out at the meadow.

"There's nothing so soul-shriveling as a female in a sulk," he said somberly.

"I'll need the car," she said icily. "I have to phone a friend today. He's expecting my call. He's in Trois Rivières. That's a place in Canada."

"He? Well . . . well."

"He," she repeated flatly. "I have to leave in a few minutes. The keys aren't on the table where they're supposed to be. Where are they, please?"

" 'Where are they, please,' " he mimicked her, to her chagrin catching exactly the note of fake hauteur in her voice.

"Are you going to tell me about the keys?" she demanded. She felt suddenly swollen with rage, huge with it, as though she would tower over him if she stood up.

"If I want to, I will," he said.

"I left the keys on the table after I drove Reverend Ross home this morning, after I brought him here because I thought you were dying!" Her voice had risen to a shout.

He looked startled, but only for an instant.

"He must have enjoyed that," he said drily. "No more satisfying meal to a pious man than seeing his worst suspicions confirmed."

"It wasn't like that! He was good and kind to me. And he was kind to you. He pitied you!"

"I don't need his pity."

"If you won't let me use the car, I'll walk to Mackenzie."

"I'll stop you from that, too, if that is what I want to do."

She started to get out of the swing. He gripped her arm.

"You're nothing!" she cried. "You're not a writer, you're just a drunk. Moonshine man! You bastard!" She was screaming.

They struggled and tumbled out of the swing. As she turned and twisted, trying to break his grip, she saw his red-rimmed eyes, his ashen skin. She was dizzy with fury. He clung to her like a limpet. She felt her own strength even as his fingers dug into her arms.

"Let me go!" she cried out.

"Not until you forgive me!" he shouted into her ear. She thought he'd gone crazy. "You will forgive me," he gasped. "How dare you not forgive me, you only just hatched, wretched girl—"

"Let me—"

"No!"

They stood facing each other. He looked as if he was going to faint. She realized, astonished, that it was she who was holding him up. Her anger left her as a fever does, with sweat on her face and a sense of weakness. She held his arms another minute until she was sure he was steady on his feet, then she let go.

"Your boyfriend can wait forever," he said. "You cannot have the car."

"I forgive you," she said quietly.

"You must mean it."

"You drink too much," she said.

He burst into laughter. "Will you believe me if I tell you I'm afraid of you?" he asked. "Would you believe it drives me to drink?"

"I don't know what I believe," she said.

"What you said was awful. Did you know you could say such cruel things to anyone? My poor Rabbit, I thought you'd fly away across the meadow, you were so wild."

"I can't talk anymore," she said wearily. He stared at her for a moment. Then he took the car keys from his pocket and put them in her hand. "Go make your phone call," he said. "But don't tell your boy how badly you treated your old father. You might scare him off."

She walked away to the car without a backward look at him.

In the lunchroom in Mackenzie, the waitress gave her change. She didn't want to talk to anyone. It was hard to believe that included Philippe. He answered on the second ring. He must have been standing next to the phone.

" 'Ye are the salt of the earth,' " he quoted, " 'but if the salt has lost its savour, wherewith shall it be salted?' "

They always paused on their walk up Mont Royal in front of the plaque with those words from Matthew; he always read them aloud to her. She couldn't smile now.

"Catherine?" he questioned. She stared at the little heap of coins on the shelf beneath the telephone, wishing it were already used up.

"I'm here," she said finally. She read a notice about a lost dog someone had tacked to the wall.

"You sound as though you wished you weren't," Philippe said.

"I can hardly stand it," she said with sudden intensity. "He drinks all the time." Anger stirred in her again.

"Leave!" he exclaimed. "Isn't your mother back in New York?"

"I can't do that. Anyhow, it's almost over. We're leaving in a couple of days."

Someone dropped a plate in the kitchen behind the counter. There was a muffled shout.

"How is it there?" she asked with an effort. "How has it been?"

"Healthy," he replied. "Boring. Logs, water, too much coffee. I quit smoking. Catherine? I've missed you."

His voice had thinned out. He had sensed her remoteness. Was there no rest from this burden of other people's feelings? And from one's own?

"What if I call you from home next week? You'll be back in Montreal. And I'll be out of this—"

"It's okay," he interrupted her. "It must be hard, not really knowing him, and the drinking. Listen. We'll go dancing. We'll run straight up Mont Royal. We'll ski in the moonlight. I will try to correct your horrible States accent—"

"Don't say any more," she begged him, close to weeping.

He was silent a moment. She heard him breathing. Then he said, "Catherine, you have a life elsewhere."

"Yes," she said. "Yes. I forgot that. We had a

fight. It's over now. So is something else." She paused. "I missed you, too."

It wasn't exactly true. She hadn't thought about him much. She had been taken up with her father. She tried to say what was closer to the truth. "I miss you now," she said.

❧ ❧

Mr. Ames was reading in the parlor.

"Any place you'd like to go today?" he asked her, almost, it seemed to her, indifferently. It had been he who had always suggested what they would do, where they would go.

"No . . . let's stay here," she answered.

They avoided each other's company all day. If he walked into the kitchen and found her making a sandwich, he left at once. She went upstairs and stayed in her room while he was in the parlor. She took a long walk. When she returned, the car was gone.

She told herself she didn't care if he came back with a bottle of liquor. But what if he got so drunk he couldn't drive them away from this cramped, dark little house? She felt momentary panic. Well, she would walk to Mackenzie. There would be a bus to Halifax. She could walk and ride and find her way home. She took her suitcase from beneath her bed and put a few things in it and felt better for a while.

Then she felt worse. She wasn't angry anymore; she couldn't pretend to be. It was only that she couldn't believe what he said. She had always believed him—even when the steamer trunk didn't arrive and the trips to faraway places didn't materialize. She roamed through the house. What was it she had believed? She sat down on the hard little sofa in the parlor and stared at the armchair in which he usually sat. She had believed herself to be central to his life.

But she wasn't. Her father, too, had a life elsewhere.

When he came back, he was carrying a bag of groceries, which he handed over to her, asking her to put things away. She understood at once that he wanted her to see there were no bottles of liquor hidden in the bag.

She stayed in her room while he fixed supper. When he called her to the kitchen, she noticed he had used one frying pan. There was none of the usual disorder that accompanied his cooking.

He had fried pork chops and opened a jar of applesauce. There was a salad of rusty lettuce and hard pieces of tomato. Looking across the table at him as

he ate, she felt this disagreeable supper was not re-
venge for what she had said to him but the expression
of his dejection.

They had made up. But even so, there were con-
sequences.

He left her to the dishes. The glasses they drank
from were old grape-jelly jars; the flatware was tinny,
bent. Most of the dishes were cracked and stained.
She had not paid attention to these details until now.

She sat with him in the parlor. He spoke in a
rather finicking way about which route to Portland
they should take. He sighed as if it were too much
for him. He'd look at the map again. Perhaps he
ought to have the car checked, at least have the spare
tire looked at.

She must have had a strange expression on her
face. "Life's not all grand opera," he said gruffly.
She started to protest that she hadn't said it was,
but she let it go.

"I'm going to Lunenberg tomorrow morning to
look for a present for Mrs. Landy's son. I couldn't
find anything in Mackenzie. You can go with me—
or not," he said.

They had both stood up, and they seemed to her
to be too large for that dinky parlor. And then she
thought, no, it wasn't that they were too big; it was
the strain between them.

"Mrs. Landy has been very kind to us, very patient," he said.

Was there an accusation in his voice? She, after all, had not been patient with him, or kindly. But how could he be so unreasonable as to expect patience, and kindness?

"And I guess I wasn't kind!" she burst out, wishing at once she'd choked off her words.

"Oh, my dear!" he exclaimed. "No one has been kinder to me than you! I've made you so suspicious. Listen. No, don't listen. Go to bed. Go to sleep."

She sat for a while at the window in her room. The dirt road was ash-white in the moonlight; the hills in the distance loomed larger, more mysteriously than they did in daylight.

She had not thought before whether or not she had liked her mother. Her mother was one with the air she breathed, the ground she walked upon, the four corners of the world in which she moved. She had hated her at times—or felt what she imagined was hatred. Perhaps it had been hatred of the captive years of her childhood. Was growing up escaping captivity? Doing what you thought you wanted to do, when you wanted to do it? Drinking yourself into insensibility? "They think it's their own will," Ross had said, of drunkards. He had meant that will had nothing to do with it. Her head was beginning to ache.

She had disliked her father that day. Yet she did love him. She went to her bed and hit the pillow hard. Love, love, love, everyone was always saying. As though it were the easiest thing!

The words she had shouted at him in the swing came back to her. Her father had been right; she hadn't known she had it in her to be so mean. Move over, Harriet Blacking, she said to herself.

❧ ❧ ❧ ❧ ❧ ❧ ❧ Eight

WHILE CATHERINE was dressing the next morning she heard the door close below. She bent to look out of the window and saw her father walking slowly toward the car, his hands in his pockets, his head bowed.

"Wait!" she called down. She stepped into her moccasins, ran downstairs and into the kitchen, and gulped down some tomato juice. She knew she'd slept hard; sleep lingered in her heavy limbs, in the way she found herself staring at things without knowing what they were.

He'd left the car door open for her. She slipped in beside him.

"I'm here," she said.

He smiled. "So I see," he said.

They spoke hardly at all during the drive to Lunenberg, and when they did, one or the other would point out something in the countryside—a tiny, fenced cemetery in the middle of a plowed field, a tree struck by lightning, one of its main branches nearly ripped from the trunk, an elderly couple hoeing in their patch of garden, their heads wrapped in identical blue bandannas.

There wasn't much traffic in Lunenberg, but he grew nervous; his hands clenched the wheel, and she saw sweat break out on his forehead when he edged the car into a parking place large enough for a bus.

"Phew!" he exclaimed. "My life would have been different if the internal combustion machine had not been invented. Oh, for horse and buggy days! My old man told me that when he was a boy, he was taken on holiday to the Adirondacks in a coach drawn by two horses."

They walked down the street past old dark brick

buildings and new storefronts. Through an alley, she caught sight of fishing boats at rest on the bright blue water of Lunenberg Bay.

"You never told me about him," she said. "Or about her, my grandmother."

"Your grandmother," he said musingly. "She would have gone to any length to avoid being a grandmother—and in fact she did go to an extreme length. I think she died young to avoid suffering the indignities and changes of age. As for him, he had beautiful red hair. He had studied philosophy in a German university, but he made his living as a salesman. In his day, salesmen were called drummers. He had to travel a good deal. I didn't like him to go away. The house was very silent when he was gone. One day when he was setting off with his salesman's black case of pharmaceuticals—that's what he sold —how well I remember that black case, I hated it so—I hid behind a tree. When he walked down to his car, I threw an apple core at him and shouted, 'Red! Red!' I remember so well how he threw back his head and laughed. He didn't do that often. That's enough about him."

"It's not enough," she murmured.

"I have some old photos," he said. "I'll send them along to you."

She was puzzled by his reluctance. He would talk about anything, as a rule. But she sensed she wouldn't be able to get much more out of him on the subject of his parents.

"Where did you live when you were little?"

"Nyack," he said, almost resentfully.

"You didn't like it?"

He paused for a moment. "There was something I didn't like," he answered. "Maybe it wasn't Nyack."

They had stopped in front of the display windows of a small department store. "Come on. Let's see what we can find in here."

"How old is little Jackie?" Catherine wondered.

"Hard to guess. Mrs. Landy is probably in her forties. I have the impression Jackie is five or six."

"She never mentions a Mr. Landy."

"Perhaps he fled to the mainland."

In the store's toy section, they found a red tricycle. After some hesitation, Mr. Ames bought it, and they took it back to the car.

For a while they walked around the town. When she glanced at him, he looked as unknowable as the strangers whom they passed. She wanted very much to ask him more about his redheaded father, his mother who didn't want to grow old, the place where he'd lived as a child.

"What an odd place to be," he remarked, as they stood on a corner waiting for the traffic light to change. "For an old world traveler like myself, this humble crossroads is a sign of decline."

There were other signs of decline, Catherine thought, but she said nothing. And what was so humble about this crossroads?

They found a restaurant near the harbor, where they had a lunch of freshly caught mackerel and new potatoes.

"Isn't this wonderful?" he asked. She felt a certain tension, a fear that he would insist on her being conscious of this moment being "wonderful." He must have caught a flicker of what she was feeling, must have seen it in her face. He fell abruptly silent.

When the waiter brought him the coffee he'd ordered, he got up and said, "I'll be back in an instant . . ." and she watched him with alarm as he wound among the tables and out the restaurant door. He was going to get a drink somewhere; maybe he had noticed a bar near the restaurant. But Mr. Ames returned almost at once. He was opening a pack of cigarettes.

"I thought you were going to try and stop."

"I was," he replied. "And now I've started again. Having fun . . ."

There was a note of willfulness in his voice, even of belligerence, she had been hearing often lately. The worst of it was that he might have been speaking to anyone at all.

He inhaled deeply. "I see disapproval written all over your face," he said mildly. "Don't be a young fogy."

"But it's so bad for you," she said with urgency. He looked fragile and elderly. Yet now she thought she could see that child in him who had thrown an apple core at his father because he didn't want him to go away.

He stared at her a moment. Slowly, he ground out the cigarette in an ashtray. "If it worries you so much . . ." he said. "And, of course, you're right."

Still, when they left the restaurant, he put the pack of cigarettes in his pocket.

They spent an hour or so walking around the waterfront, looking at fishing boats. He told her how Joseph Conrad had come to the United States when he was an elderly man, "ancient by your standards," for a series of lectures. But he never got off his ship. "Life had worn him out," Mr. Ames said.

Had he invented the story? she wondered. Conrad, too, had been a traveler. But he'd not written budget travel books for tourists. She felt guilty at once. She'd kept in her memory, she was sure, everything he had ever said to her. Now she questioned what he said, secretly disbelieving.

"Let's go to a movie," he said suddenly. "Let's get out of this insistent sunlight." He grinned at her. "Come on! We'll be spendthrifts. We'll waste a day. We'll waste this glory."

She smiled because she felt obliged to smile. He was looking straight at her. He would sense any opposition. He reached out and brushed her hair behind her ears. They were standing in front of a fish market. The bellies of the freshly caught fish gleamed like wet silk. A drop of blood at the corner of the mouth of a huge silver and black fish caught her eye. She shuddered, recalling the animal skeleton in the pit in the meadow.

"Don't be scared," he said gently.

When they emerged, blinking, a couple of hours later from the movie house, he said it hadn't been much of a picture. "A really good movie is always a fairy tale," he said. "The more they try to be like life, to be realistic, the less real they are. That's a paradox. I suppose you know what that is, my ignorant child?"

"I think so," she replied. She was glad to hear him speaking in a kidding, indulgent way. He didn't press her to explain paradox. As they drove out of

Lunenberg toward the little house, she felt she was flying ahead toward her real home, a thousand miles away.

For supper that night he made a *piperade*, a Basque omelet, he told her. When they'd finished, he asked, "Shall I read to you?"

He sounded uncertain. She longed for what was ordinary, a rest from thinking, wondering. During their brief visits, she had found everything simple. At least, she had thought she had. But now, after living with her father this month, all that she had unthinkingly taken for granted was open to doubt; all certainties had shifted, broken up.

He was smoking continuously, dragging on each cigarette with a starved look on his face. When the smoke made him cough, he turned away from her as though she wouldn't hear him if she couldn't see his face.

She wanted to apologize to him for what she had shouted out in the swing. As she thought of her words, she felt their truth sink into her, blunt truths like rocks hurled. And just because they were true, because he was not the writer he had set out to be, her pity for him deepened.

"Well . . . not tonight, thanks," she said softly.

He gave her a searching look. She tried to face him openly. But the conscious effort she put into it made her feel fake. She began to clear away the dishes and stack them in the sink. She heard him strike a kitchen match to light still another cigarette.

"It hasn't worked," he said quietly. "Oh dear, oh dear. . . . Too late."

She said nothing.

"But you'll remember these days, won't you?" he asked.

When she didn't answer, he asked angrily, "Catherine? Are you a stone?"

She turned to him. "I'm sorry for what I said yesterday. I wish I hadn't said those things to you."

He sighed immensely. "Thank you for that," he said. "Someone has to forgive me. God knows, I can't forgive myself."

"I'll go pack when I finish the dishes," she said.

"Yes," he agreed, nodding. He left the kitchen. She felt peculiar for a moment, until she realized he had gone because she had dismissed him. She was glad he had. For all the pity she felt, he was a burden to her right now.

Mrs. Landy was coming in the morning and they would all three clean the house together. Then Mr. Ames was to drop her off at her house on the way to Digby. They would cross the Canadian border at Calais and drive to Portland, where she would take the Boston flight. He would drive on to Emma and his house in Rockport, and she would take the shuttle to New York after phoning her mother to give her the time she would arrive.

"Camp is over," she said aloud.

🐝 🐝

She got up the next morning in a school mood, aware of work ahead, not overly enthusiastic, but relieved to know what she was supposed to do.

As Mrs. Landy sang tunelessly in the kitchen, Catherine began to gather up the old magazines and books they'd found in the parlor. She opened *Dracula* by Bram Stoker and read the first page. Her father came to stand at her side for a moment, looking down at the book over her shoulder.

"I saw a movie of it on television," she said.

"Were you scared?" he asked.

"Not much," she responded.

"That's because it happened outside you. If you read it, the horror of it grows inside . . . where all horror is. I was scared witless by it. Did you know Stoker was the manager of a famous actor of that period, Henry Irving? He wrote that book because of a bet he made with his brother. This was the bet—that he could write the most frightening story ever written. He won."

She put the book away on a shelf. Her heart sank. She recollected all the odd bits of information he'd given her, his stories, the news he was always bringing her about different ways to understand things. She imagined being seventeen, then twenty, and how they'd probably go back to meeting in restaurants on his infrequent trips to New York.

Then she would be gone, too, to college, or to work, to whatever was to happen to her. She could, as though they were drawn on paper, see how their paths had crossed and would now diverge. Time would make it happen. There was no stopping time. She thought of how she would probably never know him better than she did at this moment, standing in front of the shelf of dusty old yellowing books in this cramped, shabby parlor, the sunlight dappling the dusty floorboards.

She hoped he would tease her on the way back to the United States, hoped they would laugh again. There hadn't been much laughter in the last few days.

She went upstairs to check her room. Her bulging suitcase lay on the bed, a strap of her bathing suit poking out of it. Her mother could fold a blouse so that it didn't wrinkle, no matter how long it stayed packed. Catherine picked up the suitcase and carried it to the door and paused there, looking back into the room. Narrow bed, oak chest of drawers, straight-backed chair, unshaded bulb hanging from the ceiling, gray-painted floor. Tonight it would be empty.

At noon they loaded up the car. Mr. Ames placed the red tricycle on top of their suitcases. Mrs. Landy hadn't noticed it; she never appeared to notice much. She tweaked her bun of hair and looked back at the house before she got into the car.

"There's been a lot of fun in Ethel Diggs's old house, hasn't there?" she asked, with slightly more animation in her voice than usual. Perhaps she was glad they were leaving. "I tell my Jackie how you two laugh so much," she said. "And how good you cook, Mr. Ames. Mr. Landy won't fry an egg. He wants the food set down before him. He doesn't want to see an egg in its shell. He says: 'Janet, I don't want to know where my food comes from. Remember that.' "

"Some men really don't like to cook," Mr. Ames said, with jovial emphasis.

So there was a Mr. Landy, thought Catherine.

"Isn't that the truth?" said Mrs. Landy.

Perhaps because she had never been so forthcoming, Mr. Ames asked her what Mr. Landy did for a living.

"Why—he works for Mr. Glimm," she replied. "The farmer you took home in the morning after getting him so drunk. Yes, Mr. Landy's worked for Mr. Glimm for twenty-three years. And my little Jackie found them their dog. Somebody had throwed it away on the road, poor thing."

She directed them to one of a dozen or so houses, much like the Diggs house, a few yards back from the country road.

"There it is," she said. Mr. Ames stopped the car so abruptly, the tricycle slid forward. Mrs. Landy smiled placidly at Catherine over the handlebar. The engine died. There was the crack of a screen door slamming. Mr. Ames got out of the car, opened the tailgate, got out the tricycle, and set it on the ground. Catherine looked at Mrs. Landy's house. Dashing down the narrow cement path toward the car, smoking a large cigar, was a tiny man in a tiny plaid woodsman's shirt and dark blue workpants.

"Here's my Jackie," Mrs. Landy said. "He's a short-order cook over at the Blue Star cafe in Bridgewater. Took the morning off so's to meet you and Catherine, Mr. Ames."

Catherine cast a horrified glance at her father. He looked frozen.

"Daddy!" she said sharply.

"Mrs. Landy," he began, staring at her. He cleared

his throat, moved a few feet away from the tricycle. "I bought this—I didn't know—"

"Oh, is that for us?" asked Mrs. Landy. "That's so nice of you, Mr. Ames. Isn't that nice, Jackie?"

"Certainy is," agreed Jackie, in a *basso profundo* voice. "Certainy is nice to meet you."

"There's a little girl lives up the way that'll just love it," Mrs. Landy said. Jackie went to the tricycle and gripped one of the handlebars and wheeled it back and forth, smiling amiably at Catherine through a cloud of cigar smoke.

Mr. Ames said in a weak voice, "I can't thank you enough for all you've done for us, Mrs. Landy." He seemed overcome for a moment.

"It's been a nice change for Mother," said the little man in his booming voice.

"Well, you've been wonderful to us," Mr. Ames continued doggedly, staring at the side of the car. "Catherine, hasn't she been wonderful?"

Catherine nodded mutely. A hundred years had passed since she had heard Mrs. Landy say Jackie was a short-order cook.

"We won't forget you," Mrs. Landy said. "That's one thing you don't have to worry about."

Jackie had taken from her the bag of leftover groceries Mr. Ames had given her. With his free arm, he continued to hold on to the tricycle. Mrs. Landy stooped and took hold of the other side of the handlebar. They began to wheel it up the walk to their house. Jackie didn't have to bend.

"Good-bye, good-bye," called Mr. Ames as he got back into the driver's seat. He needn't have said it twice, thought Catherine.

"My God!" he gasped as they drove off. "I should have bought him a box of stogies."

Catherine let out a whoop of laughter. He laughed louder, leaning back against the seat, the car swerving down the road.

"What a fool I was!" he cried. "It never occurred to me to ask how old little Jackie was."

"But how could you have known? She always talked about *little* Jackie."

"I didn't know she meant *short*," he said.

"Stop!" shrieked Catherine.

"A short-order cook," he said.

"Don't say any more!"

"How can you be so wicked—laughing at that little fellow!"

"I'm not laughing," she protested in a choked voice.

After a while, he said, "You never know. You get a peek at someone's life—you start back in dread. Would you have guessed Mrs. Landy had so much delicacy? You know she saved us, don't you? I wouldn't put it past her to have invented a little girl up the way—just so we wouldn't be embarrassed. Embarrassed! I feel destroyed!"

"I feel mean," Catherine said. "It wasn't really funny, it was unexpected."

"Don't make excuses," he said. "There's nothing funny about the way we all betray each other. You'll laugh the same way at me someday. There will be people who'll laugh at you—like that girl, Harriet, you told me about."

"Not because I'm a dwarf," she said.

"How do you know you aren't one?"

"Harriet Blacking lives in order to get the drop on everyone. I don't do that."

"Don't say what you don't do. It'll come back at you."

She welcomed this half-lecture. She was happy they were driving together through the countryside, talking the way they used to, before the night of the bootleggers. She had thought it couldn't be the same between them again. Now it was—almost.

They stopped in St. John for an early supper. He said he wished they had time enough to visit Grand Manan Island where Willa Cather had lived. When she looked at him blankly, he began to talk about Willa Cather, about her books, about how bitter she had become toward the end of her life.

"She felt the world she knew was going, and

everything good was disappearing from it," he said. "Of course, it always is disappearing. When you begin to grow old, you suffer from change of era."

She didn't understand much of what he was saying—he seemed to be speaking to himself more than to her—but she heard wistfulness in his voice when he told her to write down the titles of Willa Cather's novels. He was asking her to remember *him*.

She was looking at him intently. He looked back at her, his usually animated features composed, still.

"Listen," he began quietly, "I don't drink like that anymore. I can't. What was at work was that law —the one that says the worst thing that can happen will happen. Of all the times I should have been sober, it was during this time with you. I hope you can believe me. No excuses. And—I hope you *do* laugh at me."

She wanted to believe him.

"Wasn't that funny—Mrs. Landy knowing about the night you drove the drunks home? It's what's wonderful and awful about small-town life. Everybody knows at least a part of everything that happens."

They spent the night in an old inn in Camden, Maine. She was so tired she hardly listened to what he was telling her about a poet, Edna St. Vincent Millay, who had spent her childhood in Camden.

The name alone ran through her mind like a lullaby as she fell asleep.

The next morning, they drove to Portland and its airport. He hardly spoke. But the long silences between them were not uncomfortable.

They parted at the airline security gate. Her suitcase trundled away, under the machine that X-rayed it. They said good-bye.

Her parents had not been married to each other for nearly all of her life. It seemed to Catherine that the divorce between them, which had taken place so many years ago, and that had been the main fact about her own life, was at last final.

She went through the electronic gate. She turned back and saw him walking up a ramp. She watched him for a moment. He walked briskly. At the top of the ramp, he stopped. He looked to his right, then to his left. He didn't seem to know where to go. She wanted to run back, to help him.

A woman's voice said roughly, "Hey! Take your bag. There's other people coming along."

❧ ❧ ❧ ❧ ❧ ❧ ❧ Nine

IN THE AIRPORTS where she waited, Catherine looked through thick glass walls at planes. "They look like big fools," her father had said of them, "bumbling around on the asphalt. But when they leave the ground, that immense striving until they're free . . . that's the lovely thing."

She had studied him like a book for a month. Her heart and mind were so strained with her effort that she was glad for this time of dullness. After she had called her mother at her office, she had stood, staring blankly at magazine covers, in the small newspaper and souvenir shops.

Her mother had started to ask her something but said, "Never mind." Catherine guessed it would have been a question about Harry Ames.

There was another, disturbing question she was asking herself. It had to do with the weeks when she waited for her father to turn up at the Dalraida School. The chances were that Madame Soule would say something to her mother at some point during the next year. Would it be better if Catherine told her first?

Day by day she had waited, hardly believing at each day's end that there had been no word from him. She had covered for him with letter tricks, with lies; she had pleaded for him with Madame Soule. For herself, too. She had been so busy at her contrivances, she had hardly considered the possibility that he might simply abandon her for the summer. That he might have fallen ill or been in an accident had not occurred to her. Perhaps she had sensed then what she knew now—he couldn't rely on himself, and no one else could, either, not for those qualities of character people summed up with the word "reliable."

He was a pained and haunted man. But did he find his life unbearable? One evening, he had whispered, "The romance of life." How could you hate your life and still say such a thing? Or had what he said been only words, intangible, and as fleeting as the flute music she had heard the night he'd finally telephoned her?

"But I heard it," she said to herself, as she pressed her face against the airplane window and looked down at Jamaica Bay. "Words and music," she said to the thousand rooftops over which the plane was now descending.

As she marched down the ramp into the waiting room in New York, she caught sight of her mother searching for her, an apprehensive look on her face. When she spotted Catherine, her face lit up.

She kept her arm around Catherine's waist, hugging her as they went outside into the humid air. "Oh, I'm so glad to see you," she said again and again, as though Catherine had just been ransomed from captivity. "I'm so glad you got back in one piece."

"Why wouldn't I get back in one piece?" Catherine asked, her pleasure in seeing her mother at once clouded. She heard the old condemnation of her father lying just below the concern in her mother's voice. " 'Round up the usual suspects,' " she muttered.

"What?" asked her mother sharply.

"A line from a movie," Catherine said.

"There's a taxi," her mother said. "The bus ride is too long. You must be tired. You can't have had much rest. I was worried he wouldn't get you to Portland today. He was always late—a matter of principle with him. Does he still drive as though he were having a fit?"

"I'll tell you all about it when we get home," Catherine said, leaning back against the sticky warm plastic seat. She did feel flattened.

"How was the Lake Country?" she asked.

"Wonderful," replied her mother animatedly. "We have pictures. It's surprising, what being in the places where the poets lived does for one. Now I know they're real. I saw the chairs they sat in. We even went to Beatrix Potter's farm—though Carter wasn't too enthusiastic. We tramped for miles." She opened her pocketbook and took something from it. "Here's one little present. I also got you a beautiful tweed jacket in Edinburgh in a shop on Princes Street."

Into Catherine's hand lying open on the seat between them, she placed the smallest bear Catherine had ever seen. It was dressed in a tiny embroidered waistcoat and a green felt jacket. Another wee creature, thought Catherine, along with the Great Illusion across the street from school and Jackie Landy. She must stop growing taller or she'd be beyond the reach of all kinds of interesting beings.

"I found that in Hawkshead," her mother was saying. "A very old lady makes those bears. Wordsworth went to school in that village, Cathy. Oh— the schoolroom! I saw his initials, *W.W.*, carved in a desk."

Catherine gazed at her mother's hand, gripping her pocketbook. It was a slender hand with a new wedding band on her fourth finger. "It's a splendid bear," she said.

"You sound like *him*," her mother said reproachfully. "*Splendid* is just what he would have said."

"Why shouldn't I?" Catherine asked tersely. "*Him* is my father."

"Catherine, I've been so worried. I hope he behaved himself. I knew, I always knew, you'd have to spend some time with him. But I hope—"

"Mom. Stop hoping. I'm here. He's not Frankenstein's monster."

"Carter was concerned, too," her mother went on hurriedly, as though Catherine had not spoken.

"What has Carter got to do with Daddy?" Catherine asked. She moved closer to the window and sat up straight and didn't look at her mother.

"I'm sorry, Cathy. We've had some uneasy moments. It wasn't only worry about your father's behavior. You and I were so far from each other, thousands of miles. Sometimes I felt each one of them."

"Okay," Catherine said. She sighed and took her mother's hand in her own.

"Carter would have come to meet you, too, but he had a preregistration faculty meeting."

"That's all right."

She dozed a while, her head against her mother's shoulder, waking now and then to the noise of traffic. Then her mother was shaking her. They were in front of the apartment house on the west side of the city, where they had lived for so many years. The elevator seemed to take forever. Catherine wanted intensely to see her room, her things, the view from the window that showed a patch of the Hudson River. The sun would set soon, the water would look like a sheet of flame.

As she closed the door behind them, Catherine felt the eerie half-silence of a city apartment, the mutter and mumble of the city outside it like a distant perpetual motion machine.

"It's nice here," she said.

"It is, isn't it," her mother agreed. "These days,

I keep congratulating myself that I held on to this place. We'd never find one like it anymore at a rent we could afford."

Her mother didn't sound as though she were congratulating herself, more as if she were defending herself.

"I can see why you must have cared about him," Catherine said. They looked at each other across the suitcase.

"Wouldn't you like to unpack and wash up?" her mother asked.

"I can see, too, why you couldn't live with him."

Her mother stared at the suitcase as though it were a compellingly interesting object.

"I'm so glad to be home," Catherine said. Even as she said it, she had a presentiment that when she went back to Montreal in a week, she would be glad of that, too.

"Me, too," her mother said, reaching across the suitcase and embracing her awkwardly.

Her father had said her mother was a daylight woman. Perhaps she was, but he left out too much. There were other things about her mother he'd forgotten, or had never known. Catherine left her suitcase where it was and went to the sofa and sat down. Her mother came and sat close to her. Catherine began to tell her about the visit, the house, Reverend Ross and the fishing day, learning to use the rifle and shooting at barns.

"He always had a streak of lawlessness in him," her mother said. "He always wanted to go against things."

Catherine went on as though she hadn't spoken. She described Mackenzie and the lovely village by the sea. The pale, uneasy face of Mrs. Conklin suddenly floated into her mind, and hurriedly, she described Mrs. Landy and the tricycle, the surprise of Jackie. She began to laugh wildly. Her mother grabbed her hand and gave her a stricken look.

"Catherine! Don't laugh like that! How can you laugh so cruelly at someone's misfortune?"

"Oh, Mom! We weren't really laughing at *him*. It was because we'd been so dumb! We'd made such a mistake—about the tricycle—thinking he was a little kid when he was just a *very* short man."

"That poor mother . . . that poor little man. . . ."

"*He* didn't think he was a poor little man," Catherine cried. "You should have seen him smoking his cigar!"

"Your father always mocked people," her mother said bitterly. "His mockery was terrible to me."

"He mocks himself, too," Catherine protested.

"Anyhow, we all laugh at each other, sometimes. Even when you feel sorry, sometimes you have to laugh."

"He made me laugh at myself," her mother said. "He made me my own enemy."

"You loved him once!"

Her mother said nothing.

"You must have loved him once," Catherine cried, gripping her mother's arm.

"I was young. I didn't know anything when I met him. I suppose he was glamorous."

"What do you know now that can change what you felt back then?" Catherine demanded.

"There are shallow reasons for feelings. And there are deep ones."

"No!" Catherine shouted. Her mother put her hands over her ears, then dropped them. "You loved him once. I know it!"

"Falling in love isn't the same as—"

"It is the same. It's all the same . . . those feelings. I watched a boy I know dance a crazy clog one night on the snow. And I loved him. I'm not going to say a hundred years from now that I didn't love him, no matter what happens!"

"Let go of my arm, Catherine. Oh, Lord! Look how he's made trouble between us! He always made trouble!"

She had not known she was as big as her mother, her arms as long, her own shoulders as broad and strong, until she became aware that she had gathered her mother up and was holding her as one would hold a child, a child who, if you let go for an instant, will run away and hide herself.

"There must have been an hour, a day, when you couldn't think about anything else," she whispered fiercely against her mother's cheek, "when you loved him!"

"All right!" her mother cried, and shook herself free from Catherine's grasp and stood up, smoothing back her dark brown hair, her fingers quickly touching hairpins that kept it so neatly coiled at the nape of her neck. "All right," she repeated quietly. "I did. And for more than an hour and a day."

"Did?" Catherine asked.

"I'm going to start supper. We'll talk more later —if that's what you're going to insist upon."

Catherine nodded. She might insist but she didn't believe they would talk later about Harry Ames. She'd gotten what she wanted from her—for now. Her mother was gazing at her with curiosity, as though she were unfamiliar to her.

"I'll unpack," Catherine said.

"The tweed jacket is hanging in your closet," her mother told her. "I'm dying to see it on you." She didn't look as if a jacket was on her mind. She touched Catherine's shoe with the toe of her own. "Okay," she said, and walked off toward the kitchen.

Catherine took her suitcase to her room. They didn't have air-conditioning, and the apartment was hot, airless. She put on the new jacket, anyhow, and wore it as she got out her old school atlas from beneath a pile of textbooks. She turned pages until she found a map of Italy. She found the places her father had spoken of that day they had gone to the fishing village—Arezzo, Perugia, Assisi. She leaned closer, looking for Sansepolcro. It was there, near Arezzo. She lifted up her hand from the page. Under it was the city of Rome.

She would go to Italy herself someday.

She began to unpack. She was not going to tell her mother everything. She wouldn't speak of her father's drinking. If her mother asked her, she would say, yes, he drank some. And she wouldn't tell anyone about Mrs. Conklin. But she knew she would have to speak of the three weeks she had spent at Dalraida when she was the only student left in a closed school.

She would do it the day before she left for Montreal. Of course, it would make trouble. Her mother would blame Madame Soule as well as her father. Catherine would have to try to persuade her that

Catherine herself was as responsible as anyone else for what had happened. She had *chosen* to wait for him, after all.

But even if she told her more than she intended to—her mother had a way of getting things out of her—one thing she would not tell her was what Harry Ames had said to her at the Portland airport.

"See you," she had said, as they paused near the electronic gate.

He leaned forward. He kissed her forehead. Then he bent his head so that his face was close to her ear.

"Not if I see you first," he whispered.